THE GODDESS

*(and I'm not talking
Marilyn Monroe, here!)*

A Novel By

Lindy Michaels

This book is a work of fiction. All names, characters, places and descriptions are a product of the author's imagination. Any resemblance to actual persons, living or dead is entirely coincidental.

Cover Design Artwork by Tiffany Miller/
TifanyMillerMosaics.com

DEDICATION

To my fabulous daughters, Erin and Shani, my wonderful granddaughters, Mia, Cierra and Zoë, Goddesses all and to my grandson, Ethan, who knows a Goddess when he sees one.

To women everywhere… you are Goddess and no, I'm not talking Marilyn Monroe, here!

To Tiffany Miller, my 'third daughter,' whom so captured the essence of the Goddess with her amazing cover art mosaic.

A special thanks to Karin Buchak for doing all the techno book stuff I would have had no idea how to do!

The Reviews Are In On

THE GODDESS !!

"I SAW IT! I LIKED IT! AFTER ALL THESE YEARS THE OLD GAL STILL HAS SPUNK!!"

The Heavenly Father
Editor-In-Chief
The Times In The Sky

"GOD KNOWS I HATE TO ADMIT IT, BUT SOCIOLOGICALLY SPEAKING, IT IS RATHER POWERFUL."

Ted, The Ambitious Angel
Associate Editor
Angel News and Heaven Report

"TRUST ME ON THIS ONE, SHE'S ONE 'MOTHER' YA DON'T WANT TO MESS WITH."

Sophie
Reviewer-At -Large
The Pagan Quarterly

INTRO TO HER STORY

Fairytale, Myth or the God's/Goddess's honest truth. You decide!

In the beginning, before God, before Buddha, before Allah, yes, a very, very long time ago, perhaps eighty thousand years ago, give or take, the folks who roamed the earth believed in something. Someone. But who?

Here's a clue. It was a time when women were the center of society. They grew sustenance from the earth. They made the clay, then turned it into plates and bowls. They domesticated animals. They discovered fire. And, most importantly, they birthed babies.

And what of the men? Their main chore was to hunt big game for the lovely dinners that

1

were cooked by the women, placed on the dinnerware the women had made by hand, garnished with the vegetables the women had grown. And for dessert, succulent apples or grapes or oranges the women had picked.

And it was a time of peace. Yes, it was a time of Matriarchal Rule. Now, for all you Debbie Doubters, way back those eons ago, later to be found by archeologists, were clay icons of a woman's form with her humongous breasts and rounded hips. No icons of men were found, just those of women. Yes! They represented the earth, Herself. Well, why not? It made perfect sense. Women burst forth with new life just the way the earth did and so they worshipped Her, The Great Mother. The Goddess. And why, because they had, indeed, become great mothers themselves.

And now a very quick history that eventually tore Her-story asunder. At first, since no one had a handle on how new life came to be and sex (pardon the expression) was a simple pleasure, it was the brothers of the mothers who became the father figures of the babies born. But sadly, as time went by, things slowly changed in the small communal tribes back then, at least, for the womenfolk.

Once men figured out how to hoist themselves onto beasts, later to be called horses, they figured out that travel was a good thing and so they galloped around from tribe to tribe marauding and doing naughty things, especially to the women and the balance of power, only in its infant stage, began to shift. Perhaps the men folks were getting a tad sick of being bossed around by women. And perhaps they were just a bit jealous that they, too, couldn't expel babies from their bodies.

Not to belabor the point, we skip now to the Greeks and Romans, who, wanting equality, came up with, yes, Goddesses, but also Gods. To begin with, the Goddesses, like Diana, Goddess of the Hunt were still mighty strong, but as time went by, the Gods became more dominate and the Goddesses not only lost their A Rating in society, but were portrayed as, well, not particularly nice. Let's face it, Juno, Jupiter's lesser half was quite the bitch!

Sadly, by now, the Great Goddess had been ousted, removed, exterminated, banished and eliminated in the hearts and minds of most living upon Her, except for a dwindling number of those pesky Pagans who still roamed Her earth.

I certainly mean not to demean those of a religious nature, but truth is truth. Yes, His story has left out Her story.

Continuing on, then came the Jews, with their one all powerful male God. And what then of the women? Well, basically, they were downgraded to being mothers or whores. They could not own property, be educated, worship with the men and their becoming second class citizens had begun in earnest. And men shall inherit the earth, or more factually, take over the earth. And so they did. Patriarchal Rule became the law of the land.

Eventually, a Jewish babe was born in a manger and when grown, disagreed with some of his religious upbringing and came up with his own philosophy and we all know what happened to him, that is, if one believes that (second) good book, which was written years and years after he was nailed to the cross. And with the rise of this new religion, women suffered more and more and it would take 2000 years before women started standing up for themselves, wanting equal rights when it came to voting, what happened to their own bodies, getting equal pay and on and on. In the 70's women thought they were making some headway, only to sadly realize in present day, (I'll not name names or any political party... you know who you are) some folks are trying to make laws that take women back to Mid-evil times. And worst yet, many are succeeding.

And what of the weakened Goddess you might ask? The truth is, all those thousands and thousands and thousands of years of being beaten down and virtually ignored, She retreated into Her cave, deep in Her earth and quite forgot Her days of glory when She was all powerful, when She was revered and respected, when women and men, too, prayed to Her for food and shelter and the good life. Oh, yes, She still had a couple of responsibilities, but the truth is, She was very, very depressed

But now things were about to change. The question must be asked, though, was the world, Her world, ready for that change?

CHAPTER ONE

<u>THE GODDESS AWAKENS</u>

The fact was, it was all because of Sophie. If one were to describe this little elder beyond elder, simply picture (quite coincidentally, name wise) Sophia of the old TV show, The Golden Girls. Sophie was golden, too. She liked to describe herself as 'eternal.' She was tiny, feisty, opinionated, but always loyal to her boss. And she was quite the snoop. What and where was she snooping, you ask? Well, life on this earth, that's where. That's right. Secretly, she had left the innards of this earth to see what was going on... on it. More specifically, on her boss. It was a culture shock for teeny Sophie and that's an understatement.   After seeing what she considered to be more than enough, and actually quite bad and horrid, she hobbled back from whence she came.   This was no easy feat, considering her age. Ancient. Actually more than ancient. She was beyond ancient.

Sophie was totally out of breath, not to mention completely outraged by the time she got to her boss's cave, deep in the bowels of the earth.   Unfortunately, it was hours before the dawning of a new day and if Sophie knew anything, she knew never, ever to wake her boss before the assigned time of waking or hell would be paid. And so she, quietly as a mouse, left the cave, collapsed at the nearest tree and caught some zzzzz's.   Considering what she had just witnessed on the uppers of the earth, she tossed and turned and thrashed and twitched for hours and certainly didn't have dreams of her favorite fluffy bunnies, she loved to dream about.

On the other hand, Sophie's boss was having Her favorite dream of those long ago days gone by. The good old days. And Her dream went thusly…

Native women, wearing animal skins as clothing, young and old, were doing their morning chores, planting vegetables into the earth, cooking venison in open pits of fire, washing clothes in the near-by babbling brook, playing with the children who splashed and laughed.

Suddenly, a woman ran out of a large cave, (perhaps the very cave She was now sleeping in) nestled in the hills, crazily making wild motions with her arms, for all to come quickly to the cave. Seeing her, the women instantly stopped what they were doing and ran toward the cave.

Inside, the only light was the blazing in the fire pit. Two women added more wood to the pit, for better lighting.

Near-by the fire was a young, naked woman, squatting, her body close to the earthen floor which was covered with a zebra skin. Grunting and straining and panting, she was getting very close to the end of her labor to bring a new life into the world. Women tended to her, wiping the sweat from her brow, rubbing her back, smiling and egging her on.

And finally, finally, expelled from her body came a child, caught with precision by a very old and wrinkled elder. After the umbilical cord was cut, with a sharp handmade tool, the newborn baby girl was placed on its mother's breast, to insure immediate bonding.

And then the old woman again took this child, not ten minutes new to this earth, in her arms and walked slowly to a primitive altar in the corner of the cave and raised the child up. Placed on the altar stood a large clay Icon, molded into the form of a woman, short twigs stuck into her head for hair, dressed in a tiny animal skin which was adorned with beads and feathers. Around the Icon's neck, a beaded necklace with a large spiral hung between her large and ample molded clay breasts.

Higher, higher the elder held the baby up and then, finally, the sacred sound of her first scream of hunger. Of life.

And as the women continued to tend to the new mother, they all rejoiced at this new life, as the old woman returned the newborn to her mother's breast, so that this new and tiny one could suckle her first taste of mother's milk.

Her eyes still closed, there was a wide smile on Her face. And who, exactly, who was this sleeping grinning woman, still in Her land of dreams? Yes, that's right. It was the Great Mother of All, Mother Earth, Mother Nature. The Goddess, Herself.

She was dressed exactly as the Icon in Her dream. Wild hair filled with leaves and small twigs. Feathers hung from Her ears. Old beaded bracelets wrapped around Her wrists. She was wearing a dirty muu-muu made of animal skins. On Her feet were filthy, heavy socks and dusty hiking boots. And hanging around Her neck, in between her massive breasts, a beaded necklace with a large spiral.

Besides Her clothing, how might one describe this once so powerful woman? Well... She's big and black. If a movie were to, one day, be made about The Goddess, Whoopi Goldberg was born to play Her, or maybe Queen Latifah!

The fire in the cave's pit was all but mere embers, now, as the Goddess continued to slumber, lying spread eagle, legs up against an ancient old wooden wheel. For a moment Her eyes fluttered open and then The Great Mother let out a loud pig sounding snort. She shivered and pulled Her blanket over Her, up to Her neck.

Two minutes later, She bolted up and rubbed Her eyes with Her grimy hands. She then dragged Herself up and stumbled out of Her cave. It was pitch dark out. Still half asleep, She tiredly passed the still sleeping Sophie and slowly hiked up the hill behind Her cave.

Once there and facing the East, at least she hoped to hell so, She looked up at Her sky. Stars were still twinkling and the moon was crescent shaped. She lowered Her head and took a deep, deep breath, then slowly, very slowly started to raise her arms. In front of Her, over Her land, a faint light started to rise from behind Her earth. The Goddess, now huffing and puffing, continued raising Her arms higher and the light rose just a tad higher and then... the light fell and it was black, once again.

'Damn!' thought the Goddess as she dropped Her tired head.

"I don't feel so good," She muttered out loud, then coughed a phlegm filled cough.

She took another deep breath and tried again. As She raised Her arms, higher and higher, this time the light, the sun also rose, higher and higher, as sweat dripped down Her face. And then, yes then, the sun crashed downward, once again.

"Oh, for crying out loud!" the Goddess cried. "Crap, crap, crap, crap!"

But She tried one more time. And this time, as She raised Her arms, She started panting and blowing out air, as if She were birthing a baby.

"Come one! Come on!" She yelled at the sun, between panting and blowing out. "Jeez! Will ya come on, already?! Come on! Get the hell up, will ya?!"

Higher and higher, Her arms raised up. Higher and higher the sun slowly rose. Panting! Blowing out! Rising, rising until finally, finally the sun rose up and up and stayed up. The Goddess looked skyward, squinting at Her handiwork. After much labor, She had birthed a new day.

And then the Great Mother fell over onto the earth, onto Herself.

"I don't feel so good," she hoarsely whispered, now totally spent.

She then clumsily turned onto Her side and struggled to sit up. Sweat poured from Her dark brow, which She wiped away with her dirty muu-muu. She looked up to the sun, again and rolled Her eyes, then finally stood up. Trying to gain some semblance of dignity, She straightened Her dress, fluffed Her wild and straggly 'afro' and started to slowly walk down the hill to Her cave.

Suddenly, out of nowhere, Sophie appeared. Yes, Sophie was the Goddess's ancient servant, had been with Her since the beginning, the very beginning. Since the Goddess had Her head down as She walked and Sophie hardly came up to Her waist, they almost collided.

"For crying out loud, Sophie, watch where you're going, will ya? You almost scared me to death!"

"Ya call this living?" said Sophie with a, don't ask why, thick New York accent. "Well, good for you, your Goddessliness. I see ya managed to get it up."

"Don't mess with me, today, Soph. I don't feel so good."

"Yeah? Well ya look like crap, pardon the expression, Your Greatness."

The Goddess hung Her head even lower.

"I don't know what's wrong with me, lately."

"Lately?! Lately?! Try more than five or six thousand years. Maybe ten. Hey! I'm old. I can't keep track of all those by gone days."

"Ooooh... Aaaahhh... Ohhhhh... I ache all over, my little Sophie."

Then the Goddess had a terribly loud and hacking coughing fit.

"I don't know, my diminutive attendant of all my needs, I just feel this, this pollution in my chest." And She coughed and coughed, again.

"Uh huh... Uh huh..." Sophie said in a doctor-like tone, as she looked her boss up and down and up, again.

"Uh huh, what?! What?!"

"Serves ya right. You're out of shape, Momma! I've been telling ya that for eons. I mean, what the heck have you been doing of late, anyway? Ooh, sorry, just had to ask, Your Earthliness"

"Doing? Doing? Whatta ya talking about? I'm the Goddess, for Goddess sake! I'm... uh... I'm always busy. I still have responsibilities, ya know!"

"Yes, yes, of course you do. But doing what? Working on some new ice caps? Oh, no, wait! They're melting. Although you have whipped up some awesome hurricanes and tornados of late."

"Those weren't my fault. Somehow they got out of control and I have no idea why. My powers must need a boost of protein or something. You know I would never harm my people, intentionally. Something's going on and I just don't know what it is." The Great Mother was close to weeping, now. "Yes, that's it! My powers, my powers have gone bonkers!"

"Listen to me, My Boss Woman, I keep telling you, but ya don't believe me. It's not your powers that have gone bonkers, it's the people! Your people! They're the ones who are out of control, because you've given up and you wouldn't believe what the consequences of that have been."

Now the Goddess was angry!

"No! I gave up nothing! They were taken from me and you know it! By Him! Him!!"

Suddenly, overcome with emotions and exhaustion, the Goddess crumbled to the ground.

"I don't feel so good. I need a nap, that's what I need." And She laid down and closed her eyes, right there on… Herself.

At this, Sophie started jumping up and down and quite frankly, started screaming at her boss.

"Oh no you don't, Great Mommy. No sleep for you until you see this!"

And Sophie sat down beside Her Greatness and whipped out her iPhone from her pocket and thrust it in front of the Goddess's eyes.

The Goddess cracked open Her right eye and peeked at the complicated technology in front of her.

"What's this?" She asked quizzically.

"Just look! At this! And this! And oh, look at that!" Sophie said as she expertly swiped the small screen to photo after photo.

Disgust was in the eyes of the Goddess.

"Oh... my... my... oh... oh my. Well, I had no idea," said the Goddess, continuing to stare at image after image.

'Oh my?! That's it? Wake up, Momma. It ain't the good old days, for Goddess sake. Although, were they ever really, really good, the old days, before the worser
days of yesterday and today?"

"Huh?" replied the Goddess, thinking Sophie wasn't making much sense at all and maybe it was she who needed a nap.

"Sorry, I'm afraid I got off on a philosophical tangent of memories of olden times and present day crap. Sorry. But listen to me! It's time for you to be heard and seen again!"

"Hmmm. Really? Ya think?"

"Yeah, I think!" screamed Sophie, almost busting the Goddess's ear drum.

"Okay. Okay. But just a little nap, first?"

"No! The world waits for no woman, even if that woman *is* the world. Strategy! We must plan our strategy for your come back!"

"But just a little itty bitty nappy, first? Please. Pretty please?" whined the Goddess like a two year old begging for just one more cookie.

"No!!!"

And with that, little, itty bitty Sophie, somehow dragged the Goddess down the hill and into Her cave, which was tough going for someone who only weighed 85 pounds while the Goddess weighed, well… more.

And they stayed in the cave for quite a long time, strategizing, with absolutely no naps allowed.

CHAPTER TWO

<u>UP ABOVE THE CLOUDS TO HEAVEN</u>

Above the earth and the Realm of the Goddess, past the trees, through the clouds, up, up, up, higher, higher and you're there. Heaven.

And what in hell does Heaven look like? Is it huge, taking up miles and acres of space above the sky? Is everyone who has ever died, walking or floating around there... well, all the good folks that Saint Peter let in, anyway? If so, it must be pretty crowded up there. Is there a humongous cafeteria where they all gather for dinner? And we're not even talking about all the angels flying around. It's obvious no one will know until they no longer reside on this good earth.

As it happened, God's office area had a lovely simplicity to it. In fact, it contained only two rooms, both painted white, of course.

The outer office was the domain of Ted, The Ambitious Angel and God's go to guy. Besides being very ambitious, as already stated in his descriptive name, he was also arrogant, anal, bossy and rather obnoxious. Think the personal assistants of Hollywood's biggest stars who think they're stars in their own right. Having delusions of grandeur might be the way to describe these folks. Ted was also rather fey, in his speech, gestures and actions, but thank God there was no prejudice, at least not in Heaven.

Ted always wore a pressed white suit. He had large, white feathered wings attached to his back and a large, white halo atop his head. He looked to be in his 20's, a young age under any standard for being the Holy Father's executive assistant.

With God's go-ahead, although God had really no idea what Ted was doing, His head angel updated the offices with the latest technology: fax and copy machines, a complicated phone system and many, many large TV monitors, so that he could see every angle of what was going on... on Earth.

On this morning, one of the big screens had a golf game on with Tiger Woods still trying to make a comeback, another, a hip club where young people were dancing to Rap music, another, the Well of the American Senate, where the Republicans were filibustering yet another bill the Democrats wanted to get through Congress for the President to sign and on another, a tape of American Idol from the night before.

Yet another screen was showing the sun rising across America in real time. Ted watched, then looked to a huge digital clock on the wall, shook his head and jotted something down on a large white pad on his desk.

His attention then went to another screen, where a fashion show was in progress, with skinny, skinny models wearing outrageous outfits most women wouldn't be caught dead in, teetering on eight inch stilettos, as they strutted up and down the long cat walk to music.

"Ooh, love the boa, Honey," Ted said out loud to the TV screen.

Suddenly, a loud, but very old voice came over the elaborate intercom system.

"Hello?! Hello?! Ted? Ted!! Are you there? Ted?! Where are you…? Ted?!"

The voice had a distinct and thick Jewish accent.

Ted rolled his eyes and pressed a button on his intercom.

"Yes, Your Holiness. I'm here."

"Ted?! Helloooo?! Is anyone there? Ted?! Ted!!! I need you!"

Ted rolled his eyes again, grabbed his large, white pad off his desk and rushed toward the huge white double doors that had a gold, wood sign stating in bold print, GOD. As Ted started to open the door, again the voice was heard over the intercom.

"Ted? Where are you? I need you!"

Inside God's medium-sized office (one would think it would be very large, ornate and filled with memorabilia of over six thousand years of collecting), it was really quite simple. The office of a seemingly humble man.

Sitting behind His white desk which was much smaller than Ted's, God was dressed in a white, long toga and white sandals. On His head was a white yarmulke. A name plate on His desk read, 'Heavenly Father.' Next to it was a signed, framed picture of the Virgin Mary holding the Baby Jesus. In a bowl were a number of ripe, red apples. Also on the desk sat a menorah.

If a movie of Him were to be made, Mel Brooks would have been perfect for the part, no doubt about it.

God continued smacking all the different buttons on His intercom/phone unit and by this point was beyond frustrated. Luckily, just then Ted rushed into the room.

"Sir, remember I told you, you have to press the button on the left to hear me? I even painted it with red nail polish, so you'd remember," Ted said in a, close to, patronizing voice

"Oh, buttons, schumuttons, red, schmed! I hate all this technology crapola!"

"I'm sure you'll eventually get the hang of it, All Mighty."

"Why can't we go back to the way it was, me just leaving my door open and yelling for you, like in the old days? This is such a confusing problem for an old man."

"Well, Your Holiness, time and new inventions march on, but I'm afraid we have an even bigger problem."

"What? A problem? And so early in the morning? Oy!"

"Well, my Father, I hate to tell you this, but the sun was late rising. Again!"

There was no way that Ted hated to tell God this. The truth was, he took great relish in it. The Goddess, in his estimation, was beyond passé and he didn't know why God kept Her around, at all. And that sniveling servant of Her's, Sonia,

Sandi, Cindy, whatever her name was, well, he considered her his arch enemy. 'Sophie, right, Sophie,' he remembered.

"Oy, again. Late, you say?" said God.

"That's right, Super-Duper Dad. I think you're going to have to do something about Her, once and for all. It's time. It's past time." Ted said, this with glee in his voice.

God suddenly looked quite frightened.

"Ah, oh, well, ah... yes, okay, I guess. I, ah, okay, I will. I'll have a little talk with Her. Yes, I will."

"Well, if I do say so, myself, the sooner the better, All Powerful. Show Her who's the boss. I know you can do it!" said Ted, hoping he was pumping up his boss to act and act now!

"Right! Right you are!"

For God, the mere thought of confronting the Goddess was beyond unsettling. They'd been around together for so many moons and She had been around for millions of moons longer than He.

When He first came onto the scene, He was quite in awe of Her and Her powers. Eventually, they settled into a relationship, not unlike that of an old, bickering married couple. And then, the more popular He became, the less She became and She fought Him on this, constantly.

Truthfully, He didn't understand why She wasn't happier to have less responsibilities with the humans down on earth, but She wasn't. It just wasn't in Her nature. And now She was shirking what responsibilities She had left, that He allowed Her to have.

'I mean, how hard was it to get the sun to come up, every morning?' God thought.

The fact was, He really believed He was doing Her a favor. Women weren't supposed to work so hard. She should take it easy, pamper Herself, soak in one of Her marvelous hot springs She had created.

'Women!' God thought to Himself, 'I guess ya can't live with them, but on the other hand, ya can't live without 'em, either.'

But now, He was forced to take action, to meet with Her and demand, yes, demand that the least She could do, must do, was to get the sun up on time. What of His world, if She didn't? He was God, for God's sake. He could do this!

CHAPTER THREE

WHAT THE HELL IS GOING ON, ON ME?

Another day, another sunrise and it was almost, almost on time. With Sophie as Her trainer, the Goddess had timidly started a gentle workout routine. To begin with, She laid on Her back and lifted each leg into the air, twice. Then She did three sit-ups. And to finish She ran in place for twenty-four seconds. And She was pooped.

"Water. Water! I think I'm gonna faint, Sophie. Water!!"

"Supreme Woman of All People and Creatures. You're never gonna be in fighting form at this rate." Sophie said this as she did twenty push-ups. "See? Easy as pie."

"Easy for you to say and obviously do. You're killing me, here. Water! Water!"

Sophie passed Her a bowl of water, which the Goddess swallowed in one gulp.

"Okay. Okay. I'm ready. Yes, I am! Just a little nappy and then I'm going up there to see if all those pictures on your phone thingy that you showed me were really real."

"What, ya don't believe me? I couldn't make this stuff up, Your Highness."

"No, no, my dear servant Sophie, I do believe you. It's just that I can't believe my world has come to this. That."

"Well, unfortunately, it has and worse. You'll see. Are ya sure ya don't want me tagging along with you? I don't want you getting lost, or anything."

"No, no, I'm sure I'll be fine."

The Goddess took a very deep breath, then coughed, then looked around to see which direction She should go in, then started on Her journey to where evil lurked.

"Ah, Goddess. Goddess! Didn't you forget something?" asked Sophie, wondering if this whole thing was a good idea, considering her boss didn't seem, well, 100%. Sophie pointed back to the cave.

"Oh, right."

And the Goddess went back into Her cave, coming out a minute later with a large animal skinned purse on Her shoulder.

"I've packed everything you'll need, Your Womanliness."

And again the Goddess started off.

"Ah, Goddess?"

"What now?!"

Sophie pointed in the opposite direction the Goddess was going.

"Oh, right. I knew that," said the Goddess, as she changed her course.

"Good luck," yelled Sophie, as Her boss walked out of sight.

Across hill and dale the Goddess trekked until She miraculously found the exact spot that Sophie had specified on her instructions. She then dragged Herself up a steep and dusty hill. And onward She went, until She was overlooking the city, which She could hardly see for all the pollution.

"How do these folks even breath," She said out loud, as She coughed loudly. "Yuck! This is definitely not the way I remember it being."

But the truth was, She had not ventured out to see what was happening on Her for a few millenniums. Thinking back, She remembered it looking like Her own realm, with its high green grasses blowing in a soft breeze, blooming flowers everywhere and pristine lakes and blue skies.

Now She saw cars and more cars on freeways and industrial smoke stacks emitting who the hell knew what.

"Icky," said the Goddess, as She continued on Her way toward some kind of enlightenment about what and why and who had done this to Her world. She passed homeless people pushing rusted shopping carts filled with everything they owned. She past streets filled with trash and graffiti, She didn't understand, painted on buildings. She saw gangs of boys looking like they were going to kill each other. She walked by rivers filled with the muck of oil spills. And She did not like what had become of Her world. Not at all.

Luckily and with great forethought, The Goddess had taught Sophie how to raise the sun in the morning and set it at night. Once, when She had been feeling especially weakened (She had fallen out of a tree while collecting oranges and was unconscious for two days), Sophie had come to the world's rescue and no one was the wiser. Now the Goddess hoped Sophie remembered how to do it.

In a noisy bar, late at night, on the small stage, a pretty young thing, clad in a barely there bikini was doing her best shimmy to rock music. In between her humongous boobs hung a small fake diamond cross.   Moving with great sensuality, she danced closer to the leering men sitting around the stage, drinking. Some stuffed dollar bills into her teeny weenie bikini bottoms. Bawdy men wolf-whistled and drooled over her as she bumped and grinded her crotch close to their happy faces.

Three of the turned-on men were Dick, Pete and John.

"Hey, gorgeous, over here. Me and my buddies have something nice for you," Pete yelled over the loud music.

"Ya know, guys, a few more weeks of doing this and it's over for me. I'll be a married man," said Dick, as he tucked a crisp five into the dancer's pants, trying for a 'feel.'

"What're you talking 'bout, Dick? That hasn't stopped us, has it, Pete?" laughed John. "You just tell the little lady you're at a late meeting."

"You know, you're right, John. What does marriage have to do with a little innocent fun, right?" laughed Dick.

Leaning over, the dancing queen continued to shimmy her bodacious, buxom bosom in Dick's face, as he stuck another bill into her top. The guys were loving it.

A black waitress, dressed in a semi-skimpy outfit and serving drinks to a near-by table was listening to the three guy's banter and she wasn't laughing. One would think these women working at a place like this would be used to, even like the men's crude attention and behavior, but this wasn't just any woman waitress. No! It was, in fact, the Goddess! That's right, She still had some magic left in Her and She knew it was time to use it and use it She would, or so Sophie had insisted She must. Truthfully, She couldn't believe She was doing this, but those were things She, obviously, would have to do if She was going to change Her world. At least, so said Sophie!

The Goddess was making Her way back to the bar to pick up more drinks when a soul song by Ray Charles came on. Without realizing it, She started moving to the music, slowly swiveling Her large hips. She was soon really getting into it.

A man who was quite drunk, at a table next to Her, took out a dollar bill from his pocket and stuck it in Her top.

"You go girl!" blubbered the man. "Maybe *you* should be up on that stage!"

For a split second, the Goddess blushed and almost thanked him, then quickly came to Her senses and gave him a dirty look... but kept the dollar.

The law offices of Harry Platt and Associates was located in the penthouse suite of a tall modern office building. Stiff corporate looking, well dressed men, holding brief- cases, walked to and fro through the huge office. Pretty young secretaries, dressed corporate chic with an air of sexiness, worked diligently at their desks.

Fantastic lawyer, Nora Abrams, who was in her late forties and dressed in a severe looking pants suit, rushed through the office hallway toward one of the inner offices.

Sitting at a desk, outside that office was a black secretary, dressed conservatively, also. Yes, it was the Goddess, again. She was pretending to type on the computer, in front of her, but She had absolutely no idea what She was doing.

Inside that office, Jeffrey was sitting at his desk, throwing a nurf ball into a small basketball hoop hooked onto a bookshelf. He was young, in his thirties and clean-cut looking.

Nora quickly entered his office, leaving the door open. When Jeffrey saw her, he abruptly stopped his nurf game and pretended to be going through some papers on his desk. He wasn't fooling anyone, especially not Nora.

"Oh, hi, Nora. What a pleasure to have you visit."

"Right," said Nora. "Listen, Jeffrey, I figured out the way you can go on the Nyland versus Hiller case. Let's get together after the board meeting and I'll explain it all to you." There was definitely a patronizing tone in her voice.

It was no secret around the office that Nora didn't like Jeffrey. She thought him to be arrogant and knew he was always kissing up to Harry Platt. Not a hard worker, he believed he could get by on his charm and good looks. And he was right. After only three years, he had already made it to Associate, same as Nora, although she had been with Harry for over twenty years.

"Hey, thanks, Nora. You're really saving my ass, here."

"And your... ass... seriously needed saving on this one," retorted Nora, seething hostility.

"I know. Really sorry, but I, I was, ah, busy on another case Harry gave me."

"Sure you were."

Watching this exchange, the Goddess shook her head, got up and started for the water fountain, down the hall and literally bumped into Nora, leaving Jeffrey's office in a hurry.

"Oh, I'm so sorry," said the Goddess.

Nora only nodded her head and quickly went on her way to the office door of the great Harry Abrams, head honcho of the law firm.

The Goddess followed behind Nora. Conveniently for Her, the water fountain was directly across from Harry's office, where Nora knocked and entered, leaving the door ajar.

"So, what do you have for me, Nora?" asked Harry, a handsome, distinguished looking man pushing sixty, sitting behind his massive, well-polished oak wood desk.

"Just wanted to let you know I closed the Maynard deal, in our favor, of course. It took a lot of wrangling, but I did it."

"You're my gal! Fill me in on the details at the meeting, but good job."

Harry's phone rang and he waved Nora away, as he picked it up.

As Nora left Harry's office, the Goddess bent Her head down and took another drink of water, then walked back to Her desk, which luckily was also next door to the boardroom.

A while later, in the boardroom, Harry, of course, sat at the head of the long, rectangular table, surrounded by Jeffrey and eight other male lawyers. They were all laughing and talking to Jeffrey.

Harry's pretty, young secretary, wearing a mini skirt, tight sweater and very high heels filled the men's water glasses. When she got to Harry, he patted her lower back, actually closer to her upper ass.

"Thanks, Sweetie. Nice outfit," the lothario lawyer told her, smiling.

Barely tolerating Harry's behavior, she managed a slight smile for him, then left the room, passing Nora rushing in. The only empty chair around the table was next to Jeffrey, so that's where she sat.

"Sorry I'm late, but just got Spector to drop the charges against Jack Rutgers," she said, out of breath.

"Good job, Nora," said Harry. "Oh and congratulate our Jeffrey. I just made him a Partner."

This news hit Nora like a bombshell. She was stunned, to say the least, but somehow managed a weak 'congrats,' while really thinking, 'That bastard! Jeffrey a Partner and not me, after all these years, after everything I've done for this firm? Bastard, Harry Platt. You're a bastard!'

Watching and listening from Her desk, the Goddess was also stunned.

By now, the Goddess was quite tired, but She had one more place to check out before She could return home, cuddle up in Her cozy cave and take a long nap. Sophie had shown her the photos and this place just might well be the worst of the worst.

A fashion show was in progress in a large auditorium. Among the society and celebrity women attending, eager to see the new fall line of one of the most famous designers in the country, was a well dressed black woman wearing a very trendy outfit. Yes, yes, no surprise, it was the Goddess.

Finally, after close to an hour of skinny model after skinny model prance down the runway, wearing crazy, outrageous clothes, they all gathered on stage to pay homage to the creator of the great fashion house of one Thomas Morley. He was in his forties, tall and tan and quite Calvin Kleinish.

Everyone in the audience and the models applauded him wildly, as he took his bows. Paparazzo's camera flashbulbs went off and the audience stood yelling things like, 'Bravo!' Brilliant line!' 'Genius!' and on and on. All, that is, except the Goddess, who stood there in disbelief that this man and his clothing were considered genius by anyone with a brain or a real woman's body. Her large feet, which were stuffed into four inch pointy heels were also killing Her.

Later, in his office, Tom was happily dressing a manikin with a new creation, when Sally, his advertising executive, walked in, carrying a large manila envelope. She was reed thin and looked like a model, herself.

Entering the office right after her was a black cleaning woman, pushing a cleaning cart. Need it be said it was the Goddess? She nodded to Tom and went about her business of tidying up.

"Great show, Tom! Fantastic. I think it's your best yet!" Sally told him.

"Ah, thanks, Sal. I do what I can for the ladies."

The Goddess rolled her eyes, as She picked up some fabric off the floor.

"Well, here's what you've been waiting for. The new Thomas Morley perfume ad. You're going to love it!"

Sally carefully took three black and white large photos out of her envelope and put them on a large easel, that was standing next to the manikin.

The first photo was of a beautiful young woman with perfectly perky large breasts, wearing a sexy, see-through negligee, sitting at a mirrored vanity table, dabbing perfume on her swan-like neck.

In the second photo, the beautiful, young woman's head is turned away from the mirror with a very fearful look on her face. A beautiful young man, dressed all in black is coming toward her in a very threatening way.

And in the third and last photo, they are both naked and are obviously having sex on the chair in front of the vanity table. The young woman has a look of rapture mixed with fear on her lovely face.

Underneath the last photo reads: ATTACKED – PARFUME BY THOMAS MORLEY.

The Goddess tripped over her trash cart, trying to get a better look at the photos. She absolutely could not believe what She was seeing.

"Oh, so sorry, Mr. Morley. Just got carried away picking up some dirt."

Tom nodded to Her, then said, "I love it, Sally. But those feminists groups are going to have a field day with it."

"Oh, screw the feminists. Women will love it!"

Enraged, the Goddess had to stop Herself from attacking Sally.

"This ad, Attacked," Sally continued, "has sexuality merged with fear. Every real woman's fantasy. Believe me, it's true."

"Well, I guess you can't go too far these days, huh?" answered Tom, admiring the photos.

"Hey, the further the better, I say," said Sally. "Truth is, the more controversy, the more press, the more they'll buy!"

"That's what I like about you, Sal. You think like a man," said Tom.

The outraged Goddess had heard enough and She pushed Her cart, noisily, out of the room.

CHAPTER FOUR

A MEETING OF THE TWO RELIGIOUS ICONS

    Finally back in Her Realm, the exhausted Goddess slept for two days straight. Unfortunately, Sophie slept in both days, also and the sun was very late rising. It was reported on the news that there had been a very strange two day eclipse of the sun that caused it. In her ancient mind and to make up for the loss of daylight, Sophie had the sun set late, also. Scientists were positive that an extended eclipse couldn't possibly be the case, but they had no rational reason for it and so, for forty-eight hours people across the globe were convinced the world was coming to an end. On the other hand, conspiracy theorists were sure it was some kind of master plan devised by either North Korea or Russia, to throw the world into chaos before attacking the United States or Europe, even though it had happened in those two countries, also. Then there were some who believed it was all President Obama's fault, proving once and for all that he really was the anti-Christ.

In the end, the ones most affected were the roosters on Old MacDonald's Farm who got a very late start with their cock-a-doodling-doings.

The Goddess, after getting Her well-earned rest was having Her morning tête-à-tête with Sophie. They were sitting having breakfast near one of Her babbling brooks, eating some Fruit Loops the Goddess had gotten while on Earth.

"Hmm, yummy, but I think I'm getting a sugar high," exclaimed Sophie, who was only used to eating nuts and fruit for her morning meal.

"Yes, no wonder my people seem out of their minds. Their bodies are filled with crap like this," the Goddess said sadly, as She stuffed another spoonful into her mouth.

"I knew it! So, so, what did ya think, Momma? Tell all!" asked Sophie.

"My dear, dear little Sophie, your photos didn't even tell half the story."

"So, whatta ya gonna do?"

"Well, yeah, been thinking and thinking about that. At first I didn't know what to do, where to start and then it came to me. I saw violence, my environment going to hell, I saw homeless folks, to mention just a few of the ills that plague my land, but I think it all begins with the women. I thought they were finally making some equality headway, but for some reason, it's like the world has gone in reverse having to do with our sex. I read in the paper while I was there, that rights they had fought for, for what goes on in their bodies and won years ago, were being taken away. Damn those Southern men in power. I couldn't believe what I read." said a very, very angry and depressed Goddess.

"Well, I can,' yelled little Sophie. "You are the Supreme Woman and as your powers were obliterated, so were women's. Like I said, it's time to get powerful again, Your Goddessliness and give back the power to all of the womanly persuasion."

"You speak the truth, my little ancient person. You're right! I shall shape myself up and then whip them into shape, although I do believe it's the men who need to be whipped into shape," said the Goddess with great passion.

"Or just whipped!!!" added Sophie. "Oh, speaking of men, I almost forgot to tell you. HE wants to see you, ASAP! I sure hope He didn't find out it was me, not you, who screwed up the sun rising on time. His little twit of an assistant, Ted, wasn't very friendly when he gave me the message."

"Ya know what, I don't care what He thinks or finds out, at this point. And don't worry about that ambitious angel, Ted. I could smush him like a bug, although as the Mother of all Nature, I would never harm a bug. Ya know what I think? I think Ted is vying for God's job, one of these days. Ha! And ya know what else, dear Soph, I'm feeling stronger by the minute. It's quite amazing that having a purpose in life, again, can do wonders for one's self worth."

And with that the Goddess did five and a half leg lifts.

"Good for you, Mega Mommy," said Sophie.

The Realm of the Goddess was lush and green. Birds sang, cricket's cricketed, animals ran around free and safe, rivers flowed, brooks babbled and flowers bloomed.

The Goddess quickly strutted through the tall grasses. She was on a mission and as she got closer to Her destination, She muttered to Herself.

"He wants to talk to me? Yeah, well, I want to talk to him. Does He even have a clue as to what's going on, on me?! I think not. He's probably too busy bossing around angels or something, waiting for people to die to see who's been good or bad!"

At the very same time, God was nervously walking quite slowly through His whiteness of heaven. He, too was mumbling to Himself.

"I'll be fine. Yes, I will. I'll just tell Her like it is. She's messing up, yes She is. I mean, I'm the boss, aren't I? Aren't I? Yes, I am. I am! And I won't be intimidated by Her, even though she's way older and bigger than me."

They met at the Line between His Heaven and Her Realm. It would be a cold day in hell before either of them would ever, ever cross that line, that precarious line between the Goddess's green and God's white. Their worlds were separate and never the twain would meet, or cross over to the other one's side.

And then, there they were, facing each other. She, looking down on Him. He looking up at Her. And that's the way the Goddess liked it.

"Uh, hello..." said God, almost meekly.

"Yeah, hello," the Goddess said back.

God took a very deep and nervous breath.

"Okay, okay… the sun was late!. There, I said it."

"And…?" replied the Goddess.

"Whatta ya mean, 'and?' The sun was late rising. And for more than one day. We can't have that! I mean, well, that's just not right. It's… it's… wrong. The sun can't be late."

"Why not? My world is going to hell in a hand basket, so who cares if the sun's a few minutes late?" countered the Goddess, knowing in Her heart, it really, really wasn't a good thing.

"Well, ha, I care. And whatta ya mean the world is going to hell? That thought is very offensive to me. Anyway, I think everything is going along fine and dandy. Yes, I do. Just the way it's supposed to, with the free will I gave those folks," God retorted with just a little defensiveness in his old voice.

"No, no, no! I was just down… up there and…"

"You what?!" God interrupted. "You're not supposed to do that, get involved with my people! Who said you could do that?" God stood on His tippy-toes so He could see Her eyes, better, thinking He would look more threatening that way.

"Hey, old man, I don't need anyone's permission. You think I'm just going to stand by while they destroy my good name, my world and themselves in the process or, or… vice-versa?"

"Listen, Goddess Mother, if they happen to make a few little mistakes down there, they'll be judged later, by me! That's my job! I won't let them through my Pearly Gates if they're really, really bad. You let them be!" God, although sounding a tad more forceful, almost fell over from all the physical exertion it took by being so forceful.

"Yeah, well, I'm taking it upon myself to see they don't make so many mistakes to begin with. They're ruining me and my good name. What do you think about that? The truth is, I've been gone way too long!" the Goddess said forcefully, back.

"Oh. Well, I thought you wanted a little time off. You were the one who left, ya know. Sort of just faded away, didn't you." It was a not a question, but a statement of God's fact and there was actual innocence in his voice.

"Are you high?! No! I was banished, ousted and eliminated and you know it!"

"Really? Naw. I don't remember it that way," said God, really meaning it.

"Then you remember it wrong, Daddy. But look out, now, 'cause I'm back!" As the Goddess said this she did a karate strike with her arms, almost hitting Him in the face.

God automatically backed up in shaking fear.

"You're, you're coming back?" He said with utter and extreme nervousness. "Ah, well, what exactly does that mean? I don't think that's a very good idea, Dear."

"Good for you! And don't 'Dear' me! Well, I'm off. Got bunches of work to do. See ya around."

And the Goddess was soon on Her way to disappearing into Her tall green grasses.

"Nooooo!!! What're ya gonna do? Where're ya going? Can't we talk about this? Come back. Come back," yelled God.

But She was gone, leaving God just standing there for a long minute, alone. And then he slowly started back through the whiteness, mumbling to Himself.

"No good. This is not good. No, not good, at all…"

CHAPTER FIVE

IT'S WORSE THAN EVEN SHE THOUGHT

The Goddess was dozing by one of Her lovely lakes, snoring loudly. She was, again, dreaming of the good old days that definitely didn't exist these days. Sophie toddled up and stared at Her, disgust on her little old wrinkled face. The Goddess's eyes remained closed.

"What're ya doing! Get up!" shouted Sophie.

The Goddess woke with a start.

"What?! What?! Uh, time for the sun to set, already? Jeez, time flies by, doesn't it?" said the Goddess feeling groggy in Her head.

She looked up at the sun, high in the sky and knew that couldn't be possibly be the case. Then She had a coughing fit.

"Why are you lying around when there's work to be done? Yeah, yeah, hurray for your talk with Him, but now it's time for action, My Lady Leader!" said Sophie.

"Okay, okay, already. I went. I saw. I confronted. I'm pooped," said the Goddess, closing Her eyes, again.

"Oh, no, you don't fall asleep, again. Now you have real work to do. Get up!," yelled Sophie.

"Gee whiz, Soph, when did you get so… so aggressive? I'm tired. Not as young as I used to be, ya know?"

"Yeah, yeah, who is? My heart bleeds for you. You gotta go up there again, see what's going on and then we'll really plan our strategy!"

The Goddess painfully got up, groaning and kvetching.

"Listen, little person, yeah, I felt pretty good saying my thing to Him, but maybe it's really not as bad as we first thought. Ya think?"

"No! I don't think! And if you believe that, then I have land in Florida and believe me, the folks in power down there, well, I'd rather have land on Mars!" It was obvious that Sophie kept up to date on all political happenings.

The Goddess starting pacing back and forth, but said nothing. She was thinking, thinking of the past, of how things used to be, back when women were respected and revered, just like She had once been. And She remembered when all women's rights were no longer and much later when they fought so hard to get their rights as human beings back. How had it happened that they had become second class citizens, again, that they had to fight, fight for equality, not unlike other minorities. But they really weren't minorities when it came to their numbers.

And now, now, at least that's what Sophie had told Her, there was an out and out war against them, by the same folks, now generations later, that was, more than not, brought forth by old, white men. Oh, yes, today they were on a war path, again, against women, from what went on in women's bodies to equal wages for equal work.

When Professor Sophie had given Her a crash course in what had happened to Her gender, Her story, She was appalled and Her blood began to boil and boil some more.

"Listen, Great Mother, yes, there are so many injustices going on in your world, today, against blacks, immigrants, gays, but ya gotta start somewhere and you were right. You must start with the womenfolk. A lot of them have been brainwashed by men, again, but I believe there's still hope!" Sophie was on a roll.

"Oh, my pookie Sophie, I just don't know. It was so much easier controlling them, no, wrong word... inspiring them when they believed in me. He told me to let them, the people, be. Maybe my time really has passed and I should just let them dig their own graves."

"Are you high, Momma? No! I don't believe you really believe that. Ya gotta *do* something! You can come back, oh Great Mother Of All Living Things, I know you can! You can make a difference. You must. If not you, then who? If not now, then when?"

"Very profound, my sly servant. I like it! Alrighty! You, my dear and trusted Sophie are an inspiration to me. Yes! I'm going back up there, just to make sure I was right, that it really was as bad as I thought it was, and if so, I shall not let them just... be! No, no! I shall *make* them be strong and wonderful, to have self worth, to fight for their equality, to take their rights back. Yes! That is my mission!"

And the Goddess trudged off with Sophie happily toddling behind Her.

Dick, from the bar, the one who stuck the five dollar bill into the bikini panties of the dancer, was standing in front of a mirror in the living room he shared with his soon-to-be bride, Julie. He smiled at his reflection, fussed with his hair, cocked his head, then smiled at himself, again.

"Admiring your good looks?" laughed Julie, entering the room.

She was young and pretty and wearing a short miniskirt, crop top which barely covered her ample breasts and high heeled boots.

"Is that what you're wearing?" asked Dick looking her over. "Sort of over the top, don't you think?"

"What, you don't like it? I just got this outfit and I love it," said Julie, twirling around. "I thought you'd love it, too. I bought it just for you."

While this scene was playing itself out, inside Dick and Julie's second floor apartment, outside, sitting high on a thick branch of a large tree, hanging on for dear life, was a tree-trimmer. Yes, it was the Goddess. Luckily, the window was open, so she could hear the going's on.

Dick continued to look his bride-to-be up and down and up again, his eyes resting on the boobs he loved to snuggle his head into.

"What?" asked Julie.

"You're half naked, Sweetie. I wanna be the only one to see that cute little butt of yours. I don't want guys leering at you," Dick told her, sounding very authoritarian.

"Hey, Dick, I've worked this cute little butt off and half starved myself to get into this shape. I thought that's what you wanted."

"Yeah, for me, not for the world to see."

He then took her into his buffed arms and started to kiss her all over.

"Oh, Dickie, I love you," mumbled Julie, between kisses.

The Goddess opened Her mouth and pretended to stick Her finger down Her throat.

"Maybe after we're married, I should get you pregnant, right away. Then I won't have to worry about guys coming onto my sexy, little baby," Dick said, as he snuggled Julie's neck.

"You're so cute when you're jealous," laughed Julie.

The Goddess couldn't believe what She was hearing. Yes, if this was any indication, Sophie was right. "Let 'em be?! What, was He nuts? I shall not let 'em be!"

She had so whipped Herself into such an angry frenzy, She lost Her grip on the branch and fell out of the tree. Splat! Although the Great Mother didn't exactly land on Her feet, She did, luckily, fall on top of bunches of piled up leaves that Dick had not yet raked away and put into the trash. She was also quite close to using some of Her magic to throw 'Dickie' into the trash.

In the underground parking lot of the office building that housed the offices of Harry Platt and Associates, Harry emerged from the elevator and walked toward his very expensive sports car. He was taking his car keys out of his pocket, when out of nowhere, Nora surprised him.

"What the hell, Nora! You trying to give me a heart attack or something?" Harry said, suddenly nervous, although he wasn't sure why.

"Heart attack? You should be so lucky," seethed Nora.

"What can I do for you, Nora?"

"Oh, what can you do for me? Well, to begin with, I want an answer as to why I didn't get that Partnership, that's due me! Jeffrey's a joke and you know it. I'm the one that's done so much, everything for the firm, not to mention being the best lawyer you have!" Nora's face was getting redder and redder as she spoke. "All the accounts I've brought in. I've saved your butt and the butts of every Jeffrey you've brought in. What kind of man are you, anyway, Harry Platt?!"

"Now, now, Dear, you're quite hysterical. Please calm down, will you?" Harry said, trying to placate her. It wasn't working.

"I will *not* calm down and I'm not 'Dear!" hissed Nora.

"Well, I think you've made that quite clear," said Harry, sarcastically.

Watching in the darkness of the garage, crouching between a new Lexus and Mercedes, dressed as a Security Guard, was the Goddess. She didn't have to strain Her ears to hear the ensuing yelling.

"You're a real bastard, Harry. So what's your excuse, this time? First I was too young. Now am I too old? Or is the real reason because I'm a woman? Huh? Can't handle that I'm your smartest attorney *and* a woman. Answer me! It's 2015, Harry, not the 1950's!"

"Enough, Nora! Get a hold of yourself or I'll be forced to call Security!"

Oh, if only, The Goddess thought, who was ready to run over and wrestle Harry to the ground.

"I did, as I always do, what I felt was best for my firm."

"Know what I think, Harry? I think you're threatened by me. Oh, the things you promised me through all these years that never happened. Well, I quit! And I'm not only not taking this lying down, I'm taking all my clients with me! I'll see you in court, Mister... that is, if you live that long, you... you... sexist pig!" Nora was well beyond seeing red, at that point.

"Don't you threaten me, Nora. See, this is exactly why I've always worried about women like you."

With that final insult, Nora turned on her heels and left.

"You're out of control, Lady, do you hear me? Out of control!" Harry yelled after her.

Hot under the collar and sweating under his arm pits, Harry got into his snazzy car and peeled out of the garage.

The Goddess struggled to stand up, looked up to Heaven and shook Her fist at... Him.

At that very moment, Ted, The Ambitious Angel, happened to be watching this scene unfold, on one of his many TV monitors. He saw the Security Guard raise her fist to Heaven and then Ted heard her say, "I hope you're watching this, old man. Oh, yes indeedy, there's much work to be done and I'm just the gal to do it! And I will do it!"

Ted's eyes widened when he realized that it was no security guard who was raising her fist and yelling at his boss. No, it was... The Goddess. Uh oh. He was about to run into his

Heavenly Father's office and spill the beans about *Her*, but God had left His office early with a horrible headache, so Ted decided, instead, he would follow the Goddess, via his earthly monitors to see what else She was up to.

Attached to the top of a building on a busy commercial street, was a huge billboard with the new "ATTACKED" Thomas Morley Perfume ad.

Down below on the street, Tom and Sally looked up, admiring it, happily.

"I smell another winner, Tom," said Sally, wide smiling and very confident sounding.

"And look around, Sal, it's already getting attention," said a happy Tom.

Yes, it was true. Folks walking by, gazed up at the three photo ad. A few young women giggled at the ad, but a number of older women had obvious disgust on their faces.

Watching the older women's displeasure, Sally verbalized her defense of her ad.

"Look at those old fogies, pretending to be so very PC. They'll probably be the first to run out and buy a bottle," laughed Sally.

"I hope so," said Tom.

A homeless woman, dressed in tatters, stood near-by, holding a cup, hopefully for some change to be dropped into it. Yes, of course, it was the Goddess.

'Boy, this stinks,' thought the Goddess.

Sally and Tom started to walk away, past the Goddess, who looked Tom straight in the eye.

"Buddy, can you spare a dime?" She asked him.

Sally gave Her a dirty look and pulled Tom away, walking faster, before he could even think to dig into his pocket for some change, which, in truth, he hadn't thought of. The Goddess looked after them, then raised one of Her arms into the air, as if hailing a cab.

Without a moment's warning, the sky grew very, very dark and there was a loud clap of thunder and then from the heavens, the rains began to rain down.

Tom and Sally ran for cover, but it was too late. They were immediately drenched through and through.

The surprised Goddess, looked up at Her still raised arm and laughed out loud.

"Cool!"

CHAPTER SIX

<u>HAVING SOME FUN NOW!</u>

The Goddess was going to head back down to Her Realm and report to Sophie, but She was having some fun now. And so, She decided to stick around a little longer to get even more ammunition against those idiots who resided on Her. Since She had been so successful at bringing on the rains, She continued to do so, day after day. Yes, it poured down, flooding the streets, with thunder crashing and lightening strikes that lit up the sky.

Luckily, the continuous downpours didn't deter Dick and Julie's wedding reception that was being held in an Italian restaurant. The happy newlyweds, along with family and friends ignored the fierce weather outside and were dancing up a storm.

A little while later, in the restaurant's men's room, Dick was, once again, admiring his handsome face in a mirror that hung over one of the sinks. His friend and bar cohort, John, emerged from one of the stalls, went over to Dick and pretended to box him in some manly ritual macho way.

"So, big man of the hour, how's marriage treating you?"

"Very funny, John," laughed Dick. "So far, so good."

"So, you're driving up to the mountains, tonight?"

"Yup! A week of skiing. Can't wait. And with this storm, the snow should be wicked good. Ya know, Julie wanted to honeymoon in Hawaii, but what can I say? I won!" And Dick laughed, again.

In one of the men's stalls, unnoticed by the two men, two legs of someone were planted on the floor, pants around the person's ankles. It was the Goddess and She was pissed.

And the rain continued to pour down at Harry's massive mansion. In his large living room a huge party was in progress. Across one wall hung a banner stating, 'CONGRATS, JEFFREY!'

Mingling among the well-dressed guests was the Goddess, dressed, Herself, to the nines, although Her spiked heels were killing Her tootsies. When a waiter passed by with a tray of hors d'oeuvres, the famished Goddess grabbed a bunch and popped them all into Her mouth, at once. More than one of them went down the wrong way and She started to choke. A nice man standing near Her, asked if She was alright, then gently patted Her back until She was able to swallow again and could compose Herself.

"Are you okay, Ma'am? I'm a doctor. I was ready to give you the Heimlich Maneuver."

"Fine, fine, thank you," the Goddess managed to say, although wondering who this Heimlich person was and what his maneuver was and would it have hurt.

The man walked away and the Goddess looked around the opulent room. She saw Harry proudly walking around his domain with his wife, Emily, greeting people.

Jeffrey was getting lots of attention, as was his pretty young thing of a girlfriend. They were both reveling in all the goodies they were receiving. It was good to be Partner.

And then... then... there was a very big commotion at the mansion's front door that got everyone's attention, including the Goddess's. One of the butlers was physically fighting with a dripping wet and wild looking woman. It was Nora!

"Madam, Madam, you can't come in here. This is a private party," the butler huffed and puffed, while trying to get out of the headlock Nora had put him in.

"Private my ass! It should have been *my* party. Now get out of my way!" she said as she let go of his head and jabbed her knee into his privates.

As the poor butler, who was actually an out of work actor and definitely hadn't signed up for this kind of thing when he took this gig, let out a howling screech, there was fire in Nora's eyes and a gun in her hand.

"Harry?! Harry, where the hell are you? You're a dead man, Platt! You rotten son of a bitch!" Nora yelled, as she ran around the room looking for him.

It was a good thing Harry's mother had long passed, because she certainly would not have wanted to have been described as such. She had been a quite lovely person while she breathed on earth and not a bitch, at all.

By now, Jeffrey was trying to tackle mad woman, Nora, but she forcefully pushed him away. All this was quite amazing, considering

Nora was only five feet three, weighing 105 pounds, dripping wet, which she definitely was.

Suddenly, brave Harry rushed to her through the agitated crowd of his friends, all of whom were backing away at the sight of Nora's gun.

"Now, Nora," Harry told her in his patronizing voice. "We can talk about this, can't we? We can work this out, Dear, can't we..."

"You had your chance, Platt," she screamed, interrupting him, "And now you've said your last 'Dear' to me! I hope the judge you face in, in that purgatory place, will send you where you belong. Hell!!"

The Goddess, watching all of this with amusement, thought to Herself, 'Feisty little devil, she is. Sort of reminds me of myself in the good old days.'

And then, with her hand shaking, with the crowd gasping, with Harry now paralyzed with fear, Nora pulled the trigger.

Silence.

Nothing. No gun shot. No dead Harry.

Suddenly, Nora started laughing, hysterically. Actually, it sounded more like a cackle. It was obvious to all, she had become a mad woman. A crazy mad woman.

"Oh, Harry, you don't think I'd be so stupid as to kill you with all these witnesses, do you? I'm a great lawyer, for God's sake! But beware, Harry. I'll get you one of these days, one way or another. You can't and won't treat me like this and get away with it."

As she continued ranting, two hefty parking attendants, who were also wanna-be actors, grabbed her from behind and dragged her out of the mansion.

Emily, Harry's devoted wife, ran up to him and hugged him tightly. As he hugged her back, his face, white as a sheet, he looked up and mouthed the words, 'Thank you, God.'

The Goddess saw him and luckily was quite adept at reading lips. She said to Herself, 'Wrong All Powerful, Harry. Wrong All Powerful.'

Dick was quite correct. The snow in the mountains was perfect for skiing. And so he made run after run on the white stuff, swooshing his way down mountain after mountain, gracefully. The sun was setting (pretty much on time), as he made his way back to the mountain lodge.

Trying to keep up with him, was a bundled up in colorful ski attire and very clumsy skier, who went over a bump in the snow and lost control of her skis, not to mention her entire body. She fell down in a heap and had a very hard time trying to get up again. It was the Goddess. Taking Her skis off, She tumbled down the rest of the large hill, trying to keep up with Dick.

In the ski lodge's lounge, Julie was sitting in front of the large fireplace. Her right leg was in a thigh to ankle cast. Other skiers walking by on their way to frolicking in the snow, looked at her sympathetically.

Dick, his cheeks ruddy red, entered the lounge carrying a hot coco and some lady's fashion magazines. Behind him limped in the Goddess, holding her skies and poles, almost tripping over them. Her wild hair was in complete disarray. Getting to a chair, near to Julie, She collapsed.

"Here you go, my princess bride," said Dick, as he handed her the coco and mags.

She looked very sad and didn't thank him, just nodded.

"I hate this honeymoon, Dick. It should be renamed 'crappy-moon.' Why couldn't we have gone to Hawaii like I wanted to?" And she started to cry.

"Come on, Baby. You had fun until you broke your leg. And you were really doing great. You're a real fast learner," said Dick, actually thinking that would make her feel better.

"I was doing great? I fell off that t-bar thing going up the first time! Fast learner, right! I didn't have time to learn anything!"

"Well, Honey, next time you should listen to me when I tell you that you have to hold on tighter and not to try and get off it before it stops."

"Like there's gonna be a next time. I wanna go home, Dick," Julie told him, between sobs.

"Don't be silly. Tell you what. I'm going to go for another run or two, then we'll have us a nice romantic dinner in our honeymoon suite, okay? Night skiing is the best," said Dick, his lack of sympathy outrageous.

"Oh, yeah, it'll really be romantic, me with a broken leg. It's not like we can *do* anything," and she continued crying.

"Come on, Julie. Stop crying. And it's okay. I don't mind. We'll make up for it when your cast comes off," said the totally oblivious new husband.

"That'll be weeks and weeks and weeks from now. I hate you right now, Dick. I really do!" sweet Julie wept.

"No, no, no you don't. Don't say that, because I know it isn't true and you know it isn't true. And think about it, this will be a fun story to tell our kids one day. Okay, gotta go." And Dick split for the slopes.

"I hate you, Dick!" Julie called after him.

'I hate you, too, Dick' parroted The Goddess, silently, who hadn't missed a word.

Suddenly, the Goddess wasn't having some fun, anymore and She decided She had had enough of these humans, at least for now and decided to split, also... for home and hearth.

Back in Her Realm, Sophie was sitting near the entrance of Her Majesty's cave, playing with a bunch of her favorite fluffy bunny rabbits, hand feeding them freshly grown lettuce from the Goddess Garden. When the bunnies had finished their lunch, Sophie cuddled them for a few minutes.

"Okay, bunnies, now go forth and multiply," she told them. "Hmm, where have I heard that before?"

Just then the Goddess jogged up, almost tripping over the bunnies, which might well have ensured they would never multiply. Then She did twenty jumping jacks in place.

"I'm impressed, Dear Leader. Getting your mojo back, I see," Sophie told her Dear Leader. "I see your energy has returned."

"Well, not completely, but I'm working on it. They need me up there, Soph and I want to be in tip-top shape when the time really comes for action!"

"So, what's the plan, Mom?"

"Not sure yet. But if it takes me thousands of eons, if it takes me one human at a time, I'm going to teach those... those ignoramuses a lesson! Now I just have to figure out how. I do have a couple of ideas I want to run by you."

"Can't wait to hear! Get down with your bad self, Momma. Raise the roof!" And Sophie lifted her wrinkled arms into the air and 'raised the roof.'

And then the Goddess put Her arm around Sophie's tiny shoulder and whispered in her ear, as they walked into Her cave. Listening, Sophie was smiling and nodding her head.

God was pacing and pacing around and around in his office. Truth was, He was getting quite dizzy. Ted paced around God, going in the opposite direction. Both were very deep in thought, so deep in thought, they almost bumped into each other.

"So, Ted, My Angel, whatta ya think She's up to?" asked God, thinking He was going to pass out.

"I wish I knew, Your Supreme Heavenliness. I wish I knew," answered Ted, hating when he didn't know everything. "But

She's been down there, cavorting with your people. I think She has some kind of a plan. I just don't know what it is."

"Then what good are you to me?! Oy, oy, oy. Well, don't just pace around me, go look on one of your TV thingidos.

"Sir, unfortunately, our satellites can't reach into Her Realm."

"Modern technology crap! What's it all good for, then? Oooh, oooh, oooh, I just have this bad, very bad feeling that life as we've known it, for all these wonderful years, is about to change. She was gone for so long. Why, why, why couldn't She just stay gone? Whatta we gonna do? Whatta we gonna do? Oy, oy," asked God, as much to Himself as to Ted. Then God had a terrible coughing fit.

"Oh, Most Powerful Person. She has nothing on you. What possible harm could She bring in Her weakened state?" But even Ted was worried. In fact, very worried.

"Easy for you to say. You youngin', listen to me! Never underestimate the power of a woman. Oy, what to do? What to do?" And God sneezed twice.

The two started pacing around the office again. With Ted deep in thought, his head lowered, he almost poked out God's eye with his halo as they paced around.

And God was right to never, ever underestimate the power of a woman, especially a pissed off woman. And if ever there could be a pissed off woman, it was the Goddess. Oh, God knew what Her wrath could bring. Yes, He did.

CHAPTER SEVEN

DON'T MESS WITH THE MOMMA!

     On a winding road in the hills above the city, Harry drove very fast around the dangerous curves. Wifey, Emily, didn't want her, still upset, hubby to go driving by himself, especially after the Nora fiasco, but Harry had kissed her on the cheek, calmed her fears and left.

     Although he had laughed off Nora's almost shooting of him, the entire episode had rattled his nerves, to say the least. Should he have made her a Partner? Considering how obviously unstable the woman was, he decided he had made the right decision. Yes, she was a damn good lawyer, albeit obviously crazy, but he would work hard to mold Jeffrey into his own successful image.

But then he kept picturing Nora's gun aimed at his head and he accelerated, his foot heavy on the gas pedal, going faster and faster.

'I hope they put her in a cell and throw away the key! Lord, I hope she doesn't represent herself in court, if she sues me. She hasn't lost a case in twenty years,' Harry thought as he continued to drive around the curves at an alarming speed.

And then, then… Harry missed a curve and lost control of his ritzy sport's car. There was beyond extreme fear on his face as he went off the hill and down, down, down.

And then everything went white for Harry.

Tom and Sally were the only ones to enter the elevator. Tom pressed the button for the twenty-third floor, where his clothing design offices were.

"Tom, I had another terrific idea I wanted to run by you. How about an 'Attacked' ad for men? It could be the exact reverse of our 'Attacked' ad for women, where a beautiful girl attacks a guy. Maybe he could be sort of nerdy looking," explained Sally. "That way just regular men would think if they used 'Attacked For Men,' they could get a beautiful girl."

"Wow, that's a great idea, Sal. Then no women could ever accuse me of being sexist. And I love the nerd concept. Yeah! I like it," Tom told Sally, happily.

They both laughed as the elevator continued going up, up and up.

And then, out of nowhere, the elevator started to shake violently. And then it completely stopped.

Both Tom and Sally grabbed onto the handles in the elevator, suddenly very scared.

"What the hell..." Tom said, his voice shaking.

"Tom, we're not moving! Why aren't we moving?" Sally was quickly near hysterical.

Tom started pushing all the elevator buttons, including the elevator alarm, but no alarm went off. Then he grabbed the elevator phone for help, but the phone was dead.

And then, then... the elevator suddenly started plunging down the elevator shaft. Down, down, down, down, faster and faster.

"We're dead," whispered Tom, in a little boy's voice.

And everything went white for Tom and Sally.

On the last day of her honeymoon, if one could call it that, Julie laid on her wedded hotel bed watching a reality show about newlyweds doing crazy things on their honeymoons. By the end of the weekly show, at least two of the six contestants decided to throw in the towel and get annulments. Watching this, Julie wept and wept.

"Maybe that's what I'll do," cried Julie out loud, as tears spilled over her lovely cheeks.

She looked down at her full leg cast and the red heart that was drawn on it. Unfortunately, it had been she who had drawn it, not Dick.

At the very same time, Dick was taking his last fast run on a mountain. He was having the time of his life, when he missed a turn and went off a very steep ridge. He flew through the air, seemingly forever. Knowing he was in deep trouble and there was nothing he could do about it, his face contorted in fear.

"Noooooo!!!!" he screamed.

And then everything went white in Dick's life.

It was dark, dark black. Blacker than black. There was a horrible creaking, crackling, sucking sound emanating from who knows where.

"What the hell...?" It was Tom's fearful voice.

"Tom? Tom?! What's happening?" It was Sally's fearful voice.

"Who's there? Hello? Hello?" It was Harry's fearful voice.

"Hey! Who's that? Where am I?" It was Dick's fearful voice.

"Hello? Is someone else there? Tom?! Is that you?" said a freaked out Sally.

"It's me, Sally? Where are you?" said a freaked out Tom.

And then ever so slowly, the black began to fade some, to a murky gray.

They, The Four, were in a dingy, dimly lit cave of days of yore. The cave was filled with stalactites and stalagmites. A whooshing sound echoed around The Four. Water tricked down the cave's walls.

Their eyes finally started to adjust to their dim and dreadful new surroundings, as they all squinted their eyes, trying to focus. And then they saw each other and all reacted in total and complete scared out of their mind's dread and non-comprehension.

"Who are you?" demanded Harry, looking at Dick, who happened to be the first one he saw.

"Me!? Who the hell are you?" demanded Dick.

"Tom? Tom? Where are we? And who are those men? I don't like this. What's happening to us?" demanded scared Sally, who now clung to Tom's arm.

"Ya think I know? I don't know," Tom said, shaking in his expensive designer boots.

Far in the distance, an earthy, hearty laughing could be heard. The Four were now more panicked than ever.

"Hey! What're you laughing at, lady?" asked, a by then, hanky-needing Harry.

"*I'm* not laughing mister! Tom? Was that a laugh?" asked a now very sick feeling Sally.

"For crying out loud, Sal, stop asking me things I don't know! I don't know! I don't know!" said a trembling Tom.

"Okay, okay, let's all calm down. There has to be a reasonable explanation for this," Harry stated, already making himself the one who would be rational and save the day. "Look, isn't that a path? I think it's a path. Maybe it'll lead us out of this hell hole."

Knowing not what else they should or could do, they followed their new leader and carefully started walking down the path, a path that seemed to take them deeper into the cave.

"Excuse me. I'm no rocket scientist, but aren't we going down instead of up?" said Dick, a tad defensively, since he was the first to admit he wasn't close to being a rocket scientist.

"He's right. I say we turn around and try going the other way." This from Tom, who always prided himself in the fact that he had a great sense of direction.

Suddenly, Sally thought she saw something.

"Wait! Wait! Isn't that a light up ahead? Tom, is that a light? I think it's a light. It's a light, right, Tom?" Sally sounded almost giddy, not to mention quite out of her mind.

"I don't know! I don't know!" Tom answered, losing patience with her.

But Sally was right. Off in the distance, in the deep passageway of the cave, there was a small purple light.

"Wait! Wait!," cried a more than before, scared Dick. 'Oh my God! Are we even alive? We're not dead, are we? Oh, no, I think we're dead. We're dead! Do ya think we're dead? Do you? Do you?"

"Hey, whoever the hell you are," yelled Harry at Dick, "get a grip! We have to think rationally. Now... the last thing I remember, I was driving fast..."

"... We were in the elevator," interrupted Tom. "I think the cable broke and..."

"…We're dead! We're dead!" interrupted Dick..

A very hysterical Sally then started rambling on and on and on and on.

"No, we can't be dead because when you die there's supposed to be this tunnel that goes up to heaven and it's filled with all our dead friends and family and they welcome us, yes, that's right and there's supposed to be a beautiful white light. You heard about that, right? Everybody's heard about the white light and the colors, lots and lots of beautiful colors and this wonderful feeling of love leading us to God… Jesus Christ, this is a filthy old cave…" And she began to howl. "Where's the love? Where's all the damn love they talk about?"

"Sally, Sally, calm down! This isn't helping. But, but you don't think we're in… you know… in the other place, do you?" said Tom, close to hysterical, himself..

Again laughter is heard by The Four, only now it was much louder. The purple light in the distance was growing brighter and brighter. Seeing this, even Harry had become a blubbering baby.

"Aren't there supposed to be angels? I don't see any angels. Where in hell are the angels?" cried Harry.

And then... then, the purple light enveloped The Four, blinding them. When they finally opened their eyes, they saw a most wondrous sight. There were tall grasses blowing in the breeze and flowers everywhere. There was a lovely babbling brook, where swans sailed on the water, effortlessly.

The Four looked around in awe.

"Wow! This is more like it. It's... it's heaven," said the suddenly delighted Sally.

Behind them they heard that laugh, again. The very laugh they had heard in the cave.

They all whipped around in unison and saw... Her. And She was holding a large, yellow legal pad.

"What the hell..." spitted out Tom.

Harry stretched himself up as tall as he could to look dominate. "Excuse me, Ma'am, I'm a lawyer and I demand to know where we are!"

"Good for you," said the Goddess. "Am I supposed to be impressed?"

"Listen, lady, I want some answers and I want them now!" No, Harry would not be intimidated by this homeless looking old woman in a dirty muu-muu and dusty hiking boots.

"That's right, we'd like to know where in hell we are!" This from Tom, who for some reason was not feeling threatened, at the moment, at least.

"Hell?! Well, I'm offended, people. Are you blind? You're in a lovely meadow, near a babbling brook, on this beautiful earth I created, just for you," explained the Goddess.

"You created? And you are who?" laughed Dick.

"Who am I? Who am I?" the Goddess said forcefully. "I am Isis, Hecate, Inanna, Ishtar, Demeter, Gaia, Lilith, Kali, Tara…"

"…Well, I never heard of any of you. Them," interrupted Dick, "except for that Ishtar and that movie sucked. It was playing on cable last year."

The other three nodded in agreement.

"Really? I thoroughly enjoyed it," countered the Goddess, strongly. "Anyway, let's get started. Just for the record, please state your first names."

Since this woman before them, whoever she was, was giving them the evil eye and considering what they had just gone through, they did as they were told.

"Tom."

"Dick."

"Harry."

"Uh huh. Uh huh. That makes sense to me. And you?"

"I'm Sally."

"So, let me get this straight. Who we have here is a Tom, Dick and Harry… and Sally. Um, Harry, meet Sally… and Dick and Tom. Gee, this is fun," the Goddess said, actually having fun.

"I already know Tom," Sally told Her.

"I knew that."

"Are you going to tell us what's going on here?" piped in a frustrated Harry.

"Well, let me put it this way, people, you're all dead meat, as far as I'm concerned!" the Goddess told them, in no uncertain terms.

"Dead? Dead?! Oh, no, I knew it!" cried Dick.

"We can't be dead. If we're dead, then, then where's God? I demand to see God!" This from lawyer Harry.

The Goddess couldn't help but laugh, quite loudly.

"We're in hell, aren't we? You're the devil, right?" said Tom, backing away from the Goddess.

"I think I'm going to faint," said Sally, leaning on Tom, having a momentary dizzy spell.

"Are all of you done? Let me introduce myself, so you'll all understand," the Goddess said, as if talking to five year olds. "I am the Goddess, Giver Of Life."

"Only God gives life, Madam! This is blasphemy! Who the hell are you, lady?" Harry stated, as if he were in court, defending the right of no separation between church and state.

And then suddenly the Goddess looked them all right in their eyes, raised Her arms and suddenly the skies went black. And then a great clap of thunder was heard. To say that The Four shook in their shoes, would be an understatement.

"Oh, yes, I forgot to mention it. I am also The Destroyer! Haven't you ever heard of the Black Madonna? Well, trust me on this one, I'm one Motha you don't want to mess with. Got that? Now! Let's get down to business! You all have been very, very bad. And you will all have to answer to me for your... badness! Come, let's take a walk." The Goddess was really enjoying Herself.

The skies cleared to a beautiful blue, again, as She started to walk along Her brook that babbled. The Four just stood there, looking at each other, wondering what they should do. The Goddess turned around and saw She was not being followed. Sadly, nothing new to Her for, at least, the last six thousand years or so.

"Walk! When I say walk, you walk!"

Scared and confused, they all quickly stepped in line and followed Her.

"So what did we do? What'd I do? I'm not bad. I'm good. I am," said Dick in a pleading voice.

"Really, Dick? You're all sexist schmucks! Sound familiar, Harry?"

Harry thought and thought, but came up empty.

"Shame on all of you. Tom, you make gobs of money designing clothes I couldn't have fit into when I was seven! Shame on you!"

"Hey, I don't make women try to fit into my clothes. If they all want to look like my models, it's not my fault," said Tom, defensively.

"Yeah and they're dying in the process!" yelled the Goddess.

"I'm just trying to make an honest living, that's all," Tom said.

"Yeah, right. And you, Harry. You're an educated man."

"I am," retorted Harry, proudly.

"So, how come you're so stupid?"

"I beg your pardon?" said Harry, totally insulted.

"You treat women like crap, patting their behinds, making goo-goo eyes at them. You didn't give your best lawyer a partnership you knew she deserved and, oh, yes, you cheat on your wife!" The Goddess was on a roll, now.

"How… how did you know that?" said a stuttering Harry. "Who *are* you?"

"Oh, Harry, I am everything and everywhere. And Dickie Boy, you go to strip joints and ogle at women, you try and rule your lovely new wife and you are selfish beyond belief. Ya should've gone to Hawaii, Bub!"

"How, how did you know all that?" sputtered out Dick. "But, but I go to church. I love my mother…"

"Really? Well, it's *this* Mother you had better learn to love, sonny. And Sally! Sally, Sally, Sally. What the hell are you doing? You're a woman, for crying out loud. Shame on you the most! How can you think so little of your own sex. Your ads aren't seductive. They're RAPE!!! 'Attacked?' What, are you nuts?"

"It's just a little ad, that's all," cried Sally. "Listen, I'm in a rat race of a business and…"

The Goddess cut her off. "And you're the biggest rat of all! Now listen people, change your ways, do you hear me? Change your ways or else… or else… well, something really, really bad is going to happen to you. Get it? Good!"

The Goddess hadn't really gotten that far in Her plan to figure out what really, really bad thing would happen to them, so She decided She had done enough, scared the crap out of The Four and that would have to make do for now. She gave them all a menacing look and simply started walking away through the tall grasses of Her meadow and then, before their eyes, ZAP, She disappeared. The Four were left standing in the high grass, speechless... but not for long.

When the Goddess returned them to their homes, they were none the wiser, although She hoped they would remember, somewhere deep in their psyches, at least some of Her random threats to them. Now She just had to come up with a plan to follow through with those threats.

CHAPTER EIGHT

TALKING WITH GOD... AGAIN

Ted really, really hated going on God's errands for Him, especially this one, but that's what executive assistants have to do. And so Ted found himself carefully making his way through the lush foliage of the Goddess's Realm, trying to maneuver his wings through bushes. Looking like a duck out of water, he kept brushing his 'white' self off in a neurotic manner. Ted hated anything that wasn't white. Unfortunately, going in person, was the only way to get messages from God to the Goddess. Luckily, he hadn't had to do it more than a few times in the last six thousand years.

Suddenly, out of nowhere popped out Sophie, Ted's nemesis.

"Well, well, well. What have we here? Watch out, Theo, we ain't got no Clorox in these them parts," Sophie laughed.

"The name is Ted, old crone!" spit Ted back.

"Tsk, tsk, tsk. Lose the attitude, Theodore! You're out of your element, here."

"Where is She? I have to talk to Her."

"Listen, Teddy, you don't give the orders here, got that?"

"Ted! Ted! My name is Ted, you little annoying person!" Ted told Sophie, seeing a big dark smudge on his white, white pants.

"Whatever, Thad. Now, what can I do ya for?"

"He and that's with a capital "H" want to see Her."

"Is that so? Well, tell Your Honor to come on down!"

"Have you no respect, whatsoever, person of pint-size proportion? He wouldn't be caught dead down here!"

"Yeah?" said Sophie, ready for a fight.

"Yeah."

"Yeah?"

"Yeah!! Now listen, you ancient, whatever you are, I said He wants to see Her. Now!" Ted was getting mighty tired of playing this game, not to mention one of Her birds had just pooped on his halo.

"I'll give Her the message. So why don't you just fly away from whence you came, now? Oh, and watch out for the snakes. They love to eat little flying insects like you." Sophie relished having these little fights with Ted.

He gave her a very dirty, yet nervous look. Then he made a mad, but careful dash out of there, leaving Sophie laughing her head off.

On the line between Heaven and Earth, the Goddess paced back and forth, of course, on Her side. She looked very, very pissed.

Finally, God slowly walked up on his white side. The Goddess immediately noticed the old man didn't look too well.

"You wanted to see me and then you keep me waiting? I don't have time for this. I'm in the middle of some very important business," the Goddess told Him.

God cleared his throat before speaking. Even She could tell He seemed very nervous in Her company and this made Her quite happy.

"I told you not to mess with my people and you're still messing with them. I saw you interjecting yourself into their lives on earth and it's got to stop!" God said, trying to sound mighty and powerful, but rather failing in both.

"You messed them up, to begin with!"

"I told you to keep your nose out of things, didn't I? Didn't I?"

"And your point is?" said the Goddess, feeling mighty and powerful, Herself.

"You're moving into my territory. Now, right from the beginning the deal was that you were supposed to work on birth, hunting and gathering... and of course, cooking. I was supposed to handle everything else," God stated unequivocally.

"No!"

The Goddess started to walk down Her side of the line. God followed Her on His side.

"No? What's that supposed to mean?" God asked, trying not to sound as timid as He felt at that moment. He also felt a not so timid sneeze coming on.

"No means no! Not maybe. Not possibly. It means no, in no uncertain terms!"

"Oh," was all God could come up with.

"Now, perhaps you can ignore them and make excuses for them, but I can't. I feel compelled to take some responsibility, here, since I gave them life, life that they're screwing up, in my estimation!" said the Goddess emphatically.

"Oy, you want to talk responsibility? Then take it! The fact is, *you* screwed up!" countered God, not quite knowing where He would take this.

"Oh, really? I didn't screw up, you did!" She wanted to add, 'Na na na na na na...' but didn't.

"Hey, you were the one who gave them natural disasters!" God told Her.

"Yeah, well you gave them war!"

'Pestilence was yours. Can't deny it, can't deny it."

"And you gave them prejudice and hate. If you don't believe me, read your own Book!" The Goddess really enjoyed that zinger.

Now God had to really think.

"Okay, okay... ah, but what about, ah, mood swings! That was definitely yours."

"Mood swings? That's the best you can come up with? What about your entries: male authority, chauvinism and ego?" The Goddess loved it when She maintained the upper hand with Him.

Then suddenly God got it. He also, suddenly, got a giant headache.

"Oh, so that's what this is all about, eh? The male/female thing? Them against them? You against me?"

"If the sandal fits. Bottom line, it's ruining life! Can't even you see that? Is that what you really had in mind? Of course it was. It was your idea that women became women from, what, Adam's rib? How insulting!"

At that, God became rather thoughtful.

"No, I guess that wasn't exactly what I had in mind, but I'm not their keeper. I gave them free will, so stop blaming *me* for all their sins."

"Then stop forgiving them so easily. And why shouldn't I blame you? I was wiped off the face of the Earth because of you, which had to take some calculated effort, considering I *am* the Earth! And the truth is, Daddy, since then, women have suffered and suffered big time and it's getting worse by the day!"

"But, but, isn't that what they wanted?" God asked Her, genuinely thinking that was the truth.

"Oh, right. Listen, we could go around and around this for ages, but I don't have time. I'm out to teach them a thing or two, before it's too late."

"But, but, it's against the rules. I demand you stop interfering with my people."

"Your people? Listen old man, don't cross me. I'm angry and frustrated and really, really pissed off. I could destroy the world with one raise of my hand, but instead, I'm going to try and right my world."

And with that, the Goddess looked down upon God, knowing that He knew that She absolutely could.

"Ya know, you didn't used to be this way. You used to be gentle as a breeze, warm as the sun and caring as the... well, you were just very nurturing. I just can't talk to you, anymore. What happened to us?" God said sadly, sniffling.

"What happened? I was stopped from talking. I was stopped from being heard. But I shall be stopped no longer! No more talk. Action! So look out, 'cause I'm back!!"

"And I thought it was women who wanted to communicate. Ya know, I'm trying, here," said God, knowing He was losing the battle with Her.

"You want communication, I'll give you some. I'm now out to turn *your* world upside down, Mister!"

"Are you threatening me? You can't do that? I'm God," said God, not feeling all that All Powerful at the moment. And He sneezed three times.

"Stand back and watch!"

"Yeah? Well... well... fine."

"Fine," said the Goddess, back at Him.

And they both turned away from each other, heading back to their homes. Then God stopped, but didn't turn back to Her.

"So, are you still cooking dinner, tonight?" He said, trying to make nice.

"Fish, fresh veggies and fruit," She said, not turning around, either.

"Fine. I'll be there."

"Fine, just don't be late," She told him.

"Fine," He said, having to get the last word in.

Yes, it was true, although they definitely had their differences, the Goddess and God had dinner together, every Wednesday night, right there on the line between His Heaven and Her Earth. They never discussed much, as happens in so many families when they get together for their weekly ritual dinners, but feast they did on the Goddess's yummy bounty, once a week, year after year after year.

In one of Her lush, dense forests, the Goddess was practicing karate moves. Her opposition, a huge tree. She kicked Her leg out, expertly. She did some chops with Her arms. With each move, aggressive sounds emanated from Her mouth. If the huge tree could have cried out loud, it would have. It was being pummeled.

She then bowed to the tree, as the tree dropped some leaves onto Her head, a few of which got tangled in Her crazy hair. She then raised Her arms up above Her head, then lowered them in front of Her, hands together and whispered, "Namaste."

She then took a very deep breath in and started to shake Her body. Shake, shake, shake, harder, harder, until Her earth beneath Her started to shake, rattle and roll. The shaking was so strong, the Goddess fell over onto the ground.

"Jeez," She said, picking Herself up.

She tried shaking again and then again She was thrown to the ground. Poor Goddess was having a terrible time controlling Her powers, so out of shape was She. But She continued to try and try. She was getting completely exhausted, but tried one more time. She shook. Her earth shook. But this time, She didn't fall over, instead She snapped Her fingers and low and behold, the Earth stopped shaking.

"Yes! I'm back! I'm really back! Well, I think I'm back!" exclaimed the delighted Mother.

Just then Sophie arrived on the scene.

"Nice earthquake! Very nice, Great Mother of Extraordinary Powers," stated Sophie.

"Thank you. Thank you very much."

"So, what's crackin', Momma?" asked Sophie.

"Just honing my skills, Soph. I talked to *them*, which was an utter waste of time, the idiots. But they won't remember. They never remember. I talked to Him, which was a waste of time, also. So now the time has come for action! No more talking. I'm feeling quite great and wonderful and fabulous!"

"Oh, and that you are, Your Womanliness. That you are. I'm ready when you are!"

"Good, my faithful friend. Very good. Even with all my powers pretty much back, it will take both of us. So, let's go, then!"

And the two marched away with great purpose.

CHAPTER NINE

LET THE GAMES BEGIN

Under the strictest orders from God, Ted had tuned all his TV Earth monitors to 'Goddess Watch.' The truth was, Ted was quite annoyed, because now he would be missing the season finales of The Bachelor, The Amazing Race, Survivor, The Voice, American Idol, The Real Housewives Of Beverly Hills, Dancing With The Stars and his very favorite, Project Runway.

In the old days, he loved to watch sitcoms like I Love Lucy, Gilligan's Island, Friends and Cheers, but these days he thought sitcoms sucked, as far as he was concerned. These days 'reality' ruled. He didn't know quite why, but he really enjoyed seeing how screwed up, ego-driven and just plain sick the people of earth were.

Ted had already seen the people the Goddess had targeted, so it wasn't hard to zero in on The Four God wanted watched. Harry the lawyer, that cute, newly married guy, Dick… oh yeah and his wife, Julie and Thomas Morley and his ad gal Sally. At least he'd be able to catch a glimpse of some of the new fashions of the day, watching them.

Monitors on and ready, now all Ted had to do was wait for some action. And he waited. And he waited. God wandered out to His outer office to catch the action, too, but thus far, there was none. Still, the two sat glued to the TV monitors.

Ted explained to his boss how the Goddess wore different disguises down on Earth, so He should be on the lookout for any big, black woman doing obvious evil. And to be on the safe side, Ted told God to also watch for tiny Sophie, whom he was sure would be working as the Goddess's accomplice in whatever She was up to.

Since God didn't want to miss anything the Goddess might do and see everything for Himself, there became a real back-up of those newly departed from Earth. Not knowing quite how to handle this overload of souls, Saint Peter herded the confused mortals-no-more into

Purgatory Housing until God made His final decision to either release them into the place where angels flew, or where that horrible three-headed dog guarded the Gates Of Hell, just in case some villainous person tried to escape the fires of Hades.

In his office, Tom was working on one of his new designs on the lovely anorexic-looking Bridget. While pinning a see-through fabric over her breasts, Tom accidentally (or was it?) pricked her.

"Ouch! You stuck me, Mr. Morley."

"Sorry, beautiful. And didn't I tell you to call me Tom?"

Bridget smiled, then put her index finger seductively into her mouth, wetting it. She then wiped the pricked breast spot with it. Looking at her finger, she saw blood.

"Ooh, I'm really bleeding... Tom," said Bridget in her best little girl voice.

Tom smiled at her, then bent over and with his lips, sucked the pricked spot on Bridget's breast. She couldn't help but giggle.

"Better?"

"Better. More, please," said Bridget coyly and with a heavy dose of sexiness.

Tom looked up at her baby blues, smiled and sucked some more.

Duane, who was Tom's assistant and yes, okay, gay, ran into the room. He had a hard time ignoring the sight of his boss sucking on Bridget's tit.

"Oops, sorry," Duane said.

Tom stopped sucking, but neither he nor Bridget seemed to look embarrassed.

"What is it, Duane? I'm busy here."

"I know, I'm so sorry, Mr. Morley," Duane said in a very agitated voice. "You're not going to believe this, Mr. Morley! You've got to see what's going on down on the street!"

"Later, Duane," said Tom, eager to get back to his sucking.

Duane trotted over to the window and looked down.

"But Mr. Morley, we're in trouble, trouble, trouble! Oh my, big trouble! I think we're in deep doo-doo!"

"Alright, alright, what is it?" said the frustrated designer.

"Downstairs, ooh, we're being picketed!" said Duane, almost crying.

Now Tom rushed over to the window to see for himself, followed by Bridget, who had stopped bleeding.

Outside the window and down twenty-three stories, they saw a good-sized crowd of women of all ages, walking around in front of

Tom's building, in a circle, holding, yes, picket signs that read, 'ATTACK THOMAS MORLEY,' 'DON'T BUY ATTACKED PERFUME,' 'MALE DESIGNER, MORLEY HATES WOMEN,' BATTERED WOMEN AGAINST THOMAS MORLEY.'

Their leader, wearing a large hat was tiny Sophie. She was holding a bullhorn and yelling through it. "Women! Women! We have picked Thomas Morley to attack to make our point! We're not young and/or skinny, are we?"

The picketing women all screamed, "NO!!!"

"And we won't be used as sexual objects in violent ads, right?" continued Sophie.

"Right! Right!!" the women echoed.

"Then let's make Morley poorly! Make Morley poorly! C'mon, women, shout it out! Make Morley poorly!"

And the women did, chanting along with Sophie. "Make Morley poorly," over and over, again.

"I can't hear you!!" screamed Sophie.

More women joined the picketers and their voices swelled, growing louder and louder, so loud that they could be heard all the way up to Tom's office.

Tom was stunned watching what was happening on the street, below. Stunned and speechless.

Just then the Goddess entered, again dressed as a cleaning lady. She headed toward the window, wanting to see how Sophie was doing.

"Shit! I don't believe this!" said a pissed off Tom.

"Oh, don't worry, Tommy, they're just a bunch of old maids," Bridget said, putting in her two sense.

"Please don't call me Tommy. My mother called me that and I hated it!" Tom told his model.

"Sorry," said Bridget, moving a step away from him.

"I don't know why, but I've had this feeling, this weird feeling lately about... something. Can't put my finger on it. I just don't remember... but something... Damn! Those bitches are going to try and ruin me. Wait 'til the media gets a hold of this. And who's that woman with the bullhorn? Is that, what's her name? I once read about her or saw her on TV or something, some crap feminist, that women's hell-raiser. Bella... Bella something," said Tom, trying so hard to remember, something.

"Who?" asked Bridget, a blank look on her face.

"Bella Abzug. No, I'm afraid she's dead, Mr. Morley," piped in the cleaning lady Goddess. "But it's obvious her cause lives on."

A very angry Ted looked at Her. "Who asked you!? Get out of here, will you?"

The Goddess nodded, hiding the smile that was dying to burst out on her face.

"I'll just clean up the mess in here, later, then." And She turned Her back to them and left, now able to smile in earnest.

"Oh, Mr. Morley, should I call your lawyer? What should we do? Look, the crowd's getting even bigger!" said the now near hysterical Duane.

And Duane was right. Down on the street the crowd had doubled, maybe tripled.

"Make Morley poorly! Real women boycott Thomas Morley! He has no respect for us real women! Let's put him out of business!" Sophie continued screaming through her bullhorn.

Now downstairs, the Goddess, still in Her cleaning lady garb, joined the picketing women, chanting with them. Her eyes met Sophie's and they gave each other the thumbs up!

Up in Ted's white office, he and God, their eyes fixed on the TV monitor showing the going's on, sat there with their mouths open.

Back in Tom's office, a disheveled Sally limped in, as quick as someone could when one of their stiletto heels had been torn off. Her designer top was also ripped and hanging out of her short pencil skirt. Her usually perfectly coiffed hair was a tangled mess.

"Have you seen what's going on down there? I was almost attacked!" Sally said, completely out of breath, as she headed for the window.

"Is that supposed to be funny?" a hostile Tom asked her.

"Sorry. My God, there are crazy, wild women down there!"

"This is all your fault, Sally! Didn't I tell you we'd have a problem with that ad?"

"Bull-pucky, Tom! You loved it and you know it. You believed in it."

Tom didn't respond to her, as he nervously continued watching the mayhem below.

Harry was sitting behind his desk, talking on the phone.

"What?... What? You can't be serious, Jeffrey. Nora's suing *me*?! Outrageous! ... Yeah, you're right. I should have pressed charges, but nice guy that I am... No, I don't care if it was a fake gun. I won't take her back! Christ, what did I do to deserve this?... Okay, get back to the office ASAP!"

Harry slammed down the phone and just sat there, fuming. "Damn you, Nora! Damn you!"

There was then a soft knock at his door.

"Come in!" Harry demanded.

The Goddess, dressed, once again, as a secretary, entered.

"Excuse me, Mr. Platt. Is this a bad time?" She asked, politely.

"Who are you?"

"Oh, I'm your temp, today."

"Temp? Where's my secretary? Is she sick? Just what I need. How long will she be out?" asked the crazed feeling Harry.

"Oh. Oh, well, I guess you didn't know," said the Goddess, loving every minute of this.

"Know what? Get to the point, lady!" Harry almost screamed.

"Well, I probably shouldn't be the one to tell you, you know, spread office gossip, but well, she quit," the Goddess said sweetly.

"What? She quit? Why? How? When? Why!!" Now Harry was incensed.

The Goddess, being a great actress, besides being the Great Mother, pretended to look very uncomfortable and said nothing.

"Tell me!!"

"Well, gee, I really hate to be the bearer of bad news, but the, well, the word in the office is… she's going to sue you for, well, how do I say this, sexual harassment…?" The Goddess added some extra sweetness to Her voice while continuing. "That's all I really know, Sir. Just that she said something about, ah, 'It's the last time that pig is going to pat my ass.'"

Harry's face turned crimson, his eyes were about to pop out of their sockets, his head ready to explode.

"I'm going to kill them, all of them! This is the thank you I get for hiring them in the first place?"

The Goddess innocently shrugged.

God and Ted, with their eyes also ready to pop out of their sockets, continued to stare at the TV monitor, their mouths still wide open.

"I've got to hand it to Her, the woman has balls," said Ted.

God said nothing.

The coffee shop was filled with their lunch crowd. Eating in a booth was sweet Julie, her leg still in a cast, sitting across from her best friend, Beth.

"So tell me, tell me, how's marriage?" exclaimed an excited Beth, waiting to hear the most intimate details.

"It's okay. Not much different than living together," said Julie, not sounding like a particularly happy newlywed.

"Yeah, but now you have that beautiful rock on your finger!"

Julie looked down at her finger and twisted the ring, around and around.

"I don't know, I just thought it would be different, you know? I thought now Dick would be more sensitive and romantic."

"What, are you kidding?" laughed Beth. "They usually are that way *before* they're married."

'I guess I thought I could change him or something," Julie said sadly.

"Well, my friend, don't give up. With a little push in the right direction, maybe he can still change."

Julie leaned across the table, closer to Beth, accidentally banging her cast leg on the table.

"Ouch! Damn! ...Listen, Beth, this is a secret, just between you and me, but I almost left Dick right after our honeymoon."

"Are you serious?" said her very surprised best friend.

"He just ruined everything for me." Julie started crying. "Skiing instead of Hawaii, my leg, everything. I sat alone in the hotel for days when he went out on the slopes. He just never thinks of me."

Just then a black waitress from Jamaica appeared at their table. No surprise, it was the Goddess.

"Isn't that the way it always is, girl? You look so sweet, you deserve better, don't ya know?" said the Goddess, who had spent weeks perfecting Her Jamaican accent.

Both Julie and Beth just stared at their waitress, not knowing what to say.

"Oh, I didn't mean to intrude, but I've had the very same problem with my... mate. They just don't listen to us, do they, now?"

"They don't!" said Julie, surprising herself that she was talking about her personal life with this stranger. "I do everything he wants, but he still bullies me into doing more of what *he* wants."

"Well, child, stop it! Maybe it's time you do something he can't do, knows nothing about, hmm?" said the Goddess, trying to make Her point, without saying it directly.

Unfortunately, neither Julie or Beth had any idea what She was talking about.

"You think about it, Dearie. Now, anyone for dessert?"

Across the street from the coffee shop, high on a scaffold, two workmen were taking down Tom's 'Attacked' ad. A number of women below were watching and cheering at the giant sign's removal.

Back in the coffee shop, at another booth, Tom and Sally were deciding what to eat, although neither had much of an appetite. Then they both looked out of the shop's window and watched Tom's perfume ad come down.

"Well, there it goes," said Tom, angry and sad at the same time.

"C'mon, Tom, don't worry. It's one ad, not the end of the world," Sally told him, trying to be optimistic.

"Right, easy for you to say. A month ago I was riding high and now some stores have actually pulled 'Attacked' off their shelves. I can't believe this. What the hell is going on in the world? I've seen worse ads on TV," said a pissed Tom.

"I'm telling you, it's just a bump in the road," said Sally. "Give it a couple of weeks and those feminists will find someone else to hit and we'll get 'Attacked' out there, again."

"Yeah, you're probably right, but…"

"But nothing, Tom. I'm here to pick you up, again. How do you like this premise? Your new Tube pants and tube tops could say, 'Get the 'skinny' on Thomas Morley Fashions. Here are some sketches I already made," said Sally as she took them out of a manila folder.

The sketches were of high fashion stick figures wearing Tom's tube pants and tops and unbelievably high heels. Tom looked them over and over.

"Okay, okay. Yeah, I like 'em. Fine, let's do it, Sal." But he wasn't overly enthusiastic, at that point, about anything.

The Jamaican waitress Goddess was suddenly standing over their table, looking at the sketches, also.

"Oh, no, no, I don't think so," She said.

Tom and especially Sally couldn't believe the nerve of this woman, intruding in such a rude way.

"Excuse me? Did anyone ask you?" asked an annoyed Sally.

"No, please, excuse me. I speak out of turn," said the Goddess.

"Yes, you most certainly do. Are you a waitress or a fashion critic?" questioned a now doubly annoyed Sally.

"Yes, sorry, it's just my... nature... to say what's on my mind. Yes, none of my business."

"You're right, it isn't," Tom told Her.

"No, I guess I was just, ah, maybe just jealous. Ya know, I could never wear such clothes, yes?"

Sally looked at Her and Her abundant rear and tried not to laugh.

"No! You certainly couldn't," Sally rudely said.

"Yes, a shame. My people, we get such joy from the eating of good food. But don't you ever make the clothes for people like me? You know, all the normal people?"

"Listen, lady, why don't you try WalMart! Could we order, now?" said Tom, losing his patience.

Without waiting for an answer, Sally said, "I'll have a mound of cottage cheese and a small side of fresh fruit."

The Goddess looked at Her watch and gave them both dirty looks.

"Oh, sorry, my shift is over."

And She walked out of the coffee shop in a huff.

"What an ass-hole," said Sally.

"I don't know, Sal. First the picketers, now her. Something weird is going on, here. Think it's all some kind of an omen or something?" asked a nervous Tom.

"Don't be ridiculous," Sally told him.

Then Sally looked around the coffee shop.

"Hey!" she yelled to a waiter at the counter. "For crying out loud, could we get a waitress, already?!"

CHAPTER TEN

THE GAME EXPANDS

God and Ted were looking very agitated, watching the coffee shop scene play out on the monitor.

"Oy, oy, and oy," said God. "Maybe it *is* an omen. Goodness, goodness gracious. Oh, my, my, my."

"An omen? Nonsense, Your Most Powerfulness," stated Ted, emphatically. "It's an aberration, that's all. She's trying to influence a few folks, that's all. Nothing to worry about, Holiest Of Fathers. She can't touch your faithful, not in a million years. And truthfully, She doesn't seem to be getting through to any of them, anyway, so you see, you have nothing to worry about…" Ted rambled on and on.

"Alright, already, Ted! You don't know Her the way I do. That's what I'm saying. She has ways, believe me. She'll get you with Her sweet, sweet fruit."

"Sweet fruit?"

"Never mind. You keep an eye on Her comings and goings and keep me informed. I don't feel so good. Think I'm going to take a nap. Oy…" God told his assistant and started toddling out of the room, blowing His runny nose as He went.

"But, Heavenly Father, it's almost time for your computer class," Ted reminded God.

"I don't want to go to school, today. I have a tummy ache."

"But you must. 'Apple' just came out with this cool new software. New ways to communicate with the masses and keep up with your world. Trust me, that's the way you can really influence your flock." Ted was doing everything he could to convince God.

"Not now. My tummy hurts. She once told me eating an apple helps with that," God mumbled, closing the door behind him.

Back in Her Realm, the Goddess and Sophie were sitting outside Her cave, sharing a snack of apples and cheese.

"Well, your Loveliness, I think we're doing real good up there!" said Sophie, taking a bite out of her red, ripe fruit.

"And we've just begun to fight, Soph! I still can't believe what my world has come to, concerning women. It's quite despicable, don't you think?" asked the Goddess. 'My poor women, they've gone through so much and it seems they take one step forward and two steps back."

"Hey, lately they've been pushed a hundred steps back, don't ya think?" said Sophie.

"You're right, my loyal servant and co-conspirator. Those old, white men have gerrymandered woman's souls, outlawing everything women worked so hard to overcome. And women, why aren't they screaming at the injustices that have befallen them? I just don't understand."

"Well, they will, Momma, when we get through with them!" Sophie told Her with confidence. "They will! They've just been lulled into complacency. That's why it's so great and wonderful that you've gained back your strength and returned, to teach them all, the women *and* the men a lesson."

"You're right! And it's all because of you, my dear Sophie. All because of you," the Goddess told her trusted sidekick.

"Thank you, my Lovely Leader. Okay, enough of this lazing around. Time to get back up there and really make a difference!"

"One more bite of my apple and we're off!" said the Goddess.

The grounds of the psychiatric hospital were quite lovely and serene, housed on an acre of park-like land. Outside, nurses were walking with patients, while others sat on benches in catatonic states, the patients, not the nurses.

Inside one of the hospital's beautifully furnished private rooms, Nora was sitting in a rocking chair, staring out the window.

The door opened and old-time psychiatrist, Doctor Freda Freuda, entered. It was Sophie, her white hair wild, a la Albert Einstein.

"And good morning to you, Nora. How are we today, today?" asked Sophie, in her best psychological voice and Austrian accent.

"Good morning, Doctor Freuda. I'm fine. Actually feeling quite fine," replied Nora.

"That's good to hear. So, tomorrow's the big day. We're letting you out of this loony bin."

"How do you do it, always making me laugh, even in my darkest hours," laughed Nora.

"Well, I do believe the dark is turning into light. Now, how do ya really feel? And I have to ask myself, why do we shrinks always ask that question, especially to folks who've been put away for three months?"

"My choice, Doctor. And the truth is, I needed a good rest. I'm feeling so much better, now."

"Wonderful. Ya know what they say, when ya fall off a horse, or in this case a 'pig,' try a llama next time. No, wait a minute, that's not right," said Sophie, trying to remember what the hell that quote was.

Nora laughed out loud again and then got serious.

"So tell me, do you think I was crazy for what I did to Harry?" asked Nora of her wise doctor.

"Of course not! But I think you're a very angry woman and why not? He deserved it. Maybe next time you'll actually use a real gun. Oh! Shame on me. No, Nora, sometimes we are pushed and pushed into that corner where we feel trapped and we have to do something extreme, just to be heard. Only now, I think you should think about getting that bastard... oops, sorry, that Harry person, in a more positive way. That would make a real statement at the injustice you've incurred."

"You've read my mind, Doctor Freuda. That's what I'm going to do. I've decided to sue that creep and all I can say is, it's going to be one hell of a day in court!"

"Oh, Nora, I believe it will. Yes, I believe it will."

Dick was sitting on his couch, watching a football game. The Sunday paper was strewn around the floor. A big bowl of popcorn sat on the coffee table in front of him. Dick took a handful of his favorite football treat, stuffed it in his mouth and washed it down with a last swig from his beer can.

"Julie? Julie!" he called. "I need another beer."

From the bathroom, Julie called back that she'd be there in a minute.

"No! No! Tackle him, you idiot! Yes! Yes!" Dick loved doing an out loud play by play while watching his favorite sport.

Julie entered the living room with Dick's beer. The cast had finally been removed from her leg.

Peeking through the window, again, sitting on a tree branch, was the tree-trimming Goddess.

Julie looked at the TV and made a face. "God, I hate football."

She handed him his beer and he took it without looking at her, his eyes never leaving the game.

"Thanks, Honey. Go, go, go, go... Oh, no! Tackled, damn it!"

Only because a quick time out was called, did Dick finally look at his wife.

"C'mon and sit down. This is such a great game, Hon. Oh, see, we got the ball, again. Run, you bastard! Oh, no, major tackle!"

On the TV screen, the quarterback on the team Dick was rooting for was being pounced on by a bunch of the opposing team.

"Eeow... Yeah, real exciting, Dick, seeing men maul and try and kill each other. Great way to spend a Sunday afternoon."

Ignoring her, Dick was totally immersed in the game.

"Can we go somewhere? For a drive or something?" asked Julie of her husband.

"Wait a second... Yes!! Huh? What'd you say?"

"Dick! I want to talk to you about something."

"Again? Come on, Jules, it's my weekend. I just want to lay back and relax. Can't you leave me be, today?"

Hanging onto the tree branch, The Goddess was making faces at Dick.

Julie looked at her husband. She was angry and hurt all at the same time. She started to walk out of the room, then changed her mind.

"Dick… I'm pregnant."

"In a second, Julie."

"No, I'm pregnant, *now*!"

Suddenly her words sank into his brain. He just stared at her. Then his eyes went from her face to her still flat stomach. Suddenly, he looked very sick. He quickly got up and ran for the bathroom and slammed the door behind him.

Not understanding his reaction to what Julie thought would be wonderful news, she followed him to outside the bathroom.

"What's the matter? Can't you even say anything to me? I'm pregnant with your child, Dick!"

And then she heard Dick puking his guts out into the toilet.

Julie looked down at her tummy and rubbed it gently. There were tears in her eyes.

Through the window, the Goddess smiled at the thought of Dick puking, while feeling terrible for poor Julie. She started to lose her balance, but clung to Her branch, not falling this time.

In a large chain department store window, located in a mega-mall, a display was coming down. It was that of Thomas Morley Fashions. Watching outside the store window were a crowd of women. They were all cheering and applauding.

Inside the store, in a good-sized corner, where normally would be filled with edgy, high-end fashions, it was eerily empty. The clothing racks were bare, holding unclothed hangers. The mannequins stood naked, their red painted on lips, smiling.

It was the Thomas Morley Fashion Center. A huge sign bearing the company's name and distinctive initialed logo of TMF lay on the floor. Next to it, also laid the large 'Attacked' Perfume ad. Spray painted across the three black and white 'Attacked' photos were the words, "Empower Yourself, Women! You Should Never Be Or Buy Attacked!"

Sally stood in the middle of the empty fashion center, looking at the depressing sight. Shaking her head and very angry, she walked over to a young salesgirl.

"Excuse me, but what happened to the Morley Collection?" she asked her.

"I don't know, Ma'am. Today's my first day on the job."

"Your manager! I want to speak to your manager! Now!' told Sally.

"Yes, Ma'am, I'll get her for you, right away," said the intimidated young thing as she scurried off.

Sally paced back and forth getting more angry and outraged by the minute. Then a large black woman walked over to her. Of course, yes, it was the Goddess.

"You wanted to speak to me?" asked the Goddess, quite nicely.

"You're damn right, I do! What the hell happened to the Thomas Morley Collection? He leased this space for two years," Sally spitted out.

"Oh, I'm so sorry, but I was sure we'd informed him. Unfortunately, his line just stopped selling, almost overnight, so all our stores decided not to carry his line, anymore. But don't worry, he'll be refunded for the rest of his lease," said the Goddess in a very business-like tone.

"What do you mean, not selling! That's crazy!" yelled Sally.

"Ma'am, I'm sorry, but you'll have to keep your voice down. It isn't good for business," said The Goddess, sweetly.

"Keep my voice down? Keep my voice down?" Sally continued to yell.

"I'll have to call Security and ask you to leave the premises if you don't."

For a moment, Sally shut up and thought. She was well aware of 'Attacked' being, well, a dud, since all the brouhaha surrounding the controversy of her ad, but Tom's clothes? 'Unbelievable,' she thought.

"I'm sure Mr. Morley can understand our concern and decision," continued Manager Goddess. "We've been getting very nasty complaints, calls and emails, women customers saying they won't frequent our store if we continue to sell his clothes." Manager Goddess actually put on an apologetic face for Sally's benefit.

"Wait a minute!" said a now really steaming Sally, "Are you telling me that you're being influenced by customers?" Even Sally knew that sounded completely idiotic.

"Well, Madam, they *are* the ones who do buy our merchandize... or not, as the case is, concerning Thomas Morley."

"This is completely outrageous! Thomas Morley is one of the world's most famous designers!"

"What can I say," She said, "other than the fact that it seems like, well, the people, the women have spoken."

"Women?!!" Sally screamed. "What do *women* know about fashion?"

Sally glared at the Goddess, nearly pushing Her aside, as she walked off in a huff.

In front of Tom's building, a number of women were picketing back and forth, holding their signs.

Inside the dimly lit Runway Auditorium, sitting alone at the end of the stage, was a very dejected looking Tom.

Sally entered from the back of the room. Seeing him, she took a deep breath and walked down to the seats below where he sat, his legs dangling off the runway.

"Hi," she said, not sitting down.

"Hi," he said back.

They sat in silence for a brief moment.

"Well, Sal, I guess the jig's up, huh? I'm just about ruined. Sales are way down, all my lines have been removed from stores. What am I going to do? I never thought it would come to this."

"I'm so sorry, Tom."

"What? No new ideas? No new ways to alienate women?" he said completely consumed with bitterness.

"That isn't fair or justified and you know it, Tom. I think up the ads, but you're the one giving me the material to work with."

"You're right. I'm sorry. I'm through, Sal. I'm through. I... we were on top of the world."

"Yeah, on top of the world. So, what are you going to do," asked Sally.

"Keep designing, I guess. This *women* thing can't last forever, ya know?" said Tom.

From the back of the auditorium there was a CRASH. It was the cleaning lady Goddess, tripping, once again, over Her cart. But Tom and Sally hardly acknowledged the noise.

"So, Tom, you're going to try and ride it out, huh?" asked Sally.

"Oh, sure. Don't worry, we'll survive this. We're a team, right?"

Sally was mute. And then...

"I don't know if I'll be able to ride it out with you, Tom. I just don't know," Sally finally said.

"What're you talking about? In a month or so this will blow over and we'll be on top, again. I have a desk full of new designs ready to go." Tom told her, trying to sound enthusiastic, trying to sound optimistic.

"I can't. I'm going to have to quit, Tom. I'm sorry."

Tom couldn't believe what he was hearing. He had given Sally her big first break when she was just starting out, and now she was going to just walk away? Just like that?

"What, I'm a little down and out and someone else came along and stole you from me?" asked Tom, already feeling heat and redness rising from his chest.

"No, I don't have anything lined up, but I have to get something while I still have some kind of reputation. You can understand that, can't you?"

Hearing that and knowing Sally's reputation with her 'Attacked' ad, the Goddess had to wonder if she'd ever work this business, again 'Well, you reap what you sow, lady,' She thought, rather happily.

No, Tom was understanding nothing of what Sally told him. What happened to sticking with someone, a friend, a co-worker when they're down and out? And Tom stared at her hard.

"So go, then. What're you waiting for? And thanks for being so loyal to me, Sal. I'll remember that. Believe me, I will," said Tom, with more hurt than anger in his voice.

Sally said nothing more, just turned around and walked out of the auditorium. She passed the Goddess, who was dusting the seats, but she didn't even give Her so much as a nod.

'Well, this is interesting,' thought the Goddess.

Later, back in Her Realm, The Goddess and Sophie were in a rowboat in the middle of one of Her beautiful, pristine lakes.

"Isn't all this more fun than a barrel full of monkeys? And wow, those folks up there really are monkeys. Actually, more like apes!!" exclaimed the little ancient.

"Actually, Soph, I find it quite interesting. They seem to turn on each other when the going gets tough."

"Yup! And the tough get going, or got going. Survival of the fittest, ya know!"

"Well, we'll just see how tough and fit they are, won't we? Although, truthfully, I'm sort of feeling badly for Tom. And poor little Julie," said the Goddess, sympathetically.

"Oh, no, no, no, no! Now is not the time to get soft and sentimental on them, Momma! They haven't begun to learn their lessons."

"You're right, Dear Sophie. You're right. Okay, break's over. Back to shore! Back to work!!"

Being equal partners, they both took up their oars and began to row and row.

Ted rewound the tape he had recorded of The Thomas Morley Fashion House's demise. Not only couldn't he believe it, he was totally depressed by it. And he knew in his heart, it was all the Goddess's and that little ancient twit, Sophie's fault.

A lover of fashion, Ted had always kept up with the evolution of the Morley fashion line. The fabrics, the skirt lengths, the colors would change through the years, but Ted believed out of all the fashion designers around, Thomas Morley was in a class by himself. And now it was dead. Morley was dead. What would Milan and Paris and New York do without Thomas Morley? What would *he* do, now? *He* meaning Ted.

And yes, Ted also did have a tiny, little crush on the gorgeous Tom. Ah, unrequited love and all that. But he would be patient, because he knew, one day, probably not for decades, but one day, Tom would show up in the land of angels. And when he arrived, perhaps he would design for Ted, a new white suit, wings and a halo, with a tad more style than what he wore now. 'An angel can have dreams, too, can't he?' thought Ted, dreamily.

The thing Ted couldn't figure out and it bugged the crap out of him, was how the Goddess was doing what She was doing. From what he and God had been witnessing on his TV monitors, She wasn't actually doing much of anything, just putting her two sense into a couple of folk's lives.

But then, suddenly, women started complaining about some innocent ad, a happy newly married wife, suddenly wasn't happy, at all and a high powered lawyer picked some guy to be Partner over a crazy woman. Ted just didn't get it. With all Her threats, how his boss had better look out, because change was coming, how She was coming back, whatever that meant, well, it was obvious to Ted, the Goddess was just all blustery talk and no action. 'Nothing to worry about,' thought Ted. 'Move along, now. Nothing to see here.'

In his office, God was sitting behind his desk, rubbing His temples.

"Oy, such a headache. Such a headache. But why? I never get headaches. I'm God, for God's sake!"

And then the old man started to think that He really hadn't been feeling very great of late. When did it start, this not feeling great? Could it be, He wondered, that it possibly had something to do with the Goddess? Straining His brain, which made His head hurt worse, He realized it did, indeed, start about the time the sun was late in rising and later when He and She had had that talk. And then the second time they talked, She had looked much better than He had seen Her in ages. She seemed more determined, more powerful, angrier. And He was more tired. So tired.

They had had such a long relationship, the two of them, although God was sure He liked Her better before, when She said less, did what She was supposed to do and was simply there... when no one really acknowledged Her, anymore. Seen, felt, experienced, but not heard from, at least not in the literal sense.

God's brain was throbbing just thinking about it, about Her. He banged on half of the buttons on his phone intercom and called, well yelled, for Ted.

It took a few minutes, but eventually Ted entered God's inner sanctum.

"You called?" Ted asked, still thinking about Tom Morley.

"You heard?! I hit the right button? Oh, goodie!"

"No, Great Goodness Of the World. I heard your screaming through the door."

"Oh. Well, you're here. My head is banging, throbbing, beating, exploding! It hurts," God whimpered.

Ted sighed, not really wanted to deal with his boss, at that moment.

"You want me to rub your head?"

"Yes, please. And my neck, too." God sounded like a five year old child.

Ted went behind God's chair and started massaging His head and neck.

'Jeez,' thought Ted. 'This definitely isn't what I signed up for.'

But he rubbed the top of God's head, being very careful not to mess around with His yarmulke. Since it was attached to God's thin, stringy white hair with bobby pins, Ted wondered if it was that which was giving his boss headaches.

"Oy, feels so good. A little to the left. More... Yes, that's the spot," moaned God.

"Ahem... Your Godliness? I think we should talk about the Goddess, you know, what we've been watching, those people She's been talking to. I still just can't quite grasp what She's doing," said Ted as he continued massaging God's head and God continued to moan.

"No talk. No talk. Rub. Rub..." said God, His eyes closed.

CHAPTER ELEVEN

TOM, DICK, HARRY AND SALLY, OH MY!

Outside her quaint house on a quiet street, Nora was gardening in her front yard. Dressed in overalls, a bandana on her head, she was planting seeds for spring flowers. Since she had been released from the mental hospital, this activity had become her favorite thing to do. It gave her peace, digging in the dirt, the earth, planting seeds that one day would grow and bloom. And she believed that she might just want to spend the rest of her days in her garden. Who needed the rat race of being a high powered lawyer, defending rich bastards trying to game the system? She had had enough.

But oh, she did love the law. Perhaps she would open up a small office where she would defend the down-trodden against the injustices of their world. Perhaps she would become an advocate for women who had been sexually abused by men and represent women fighting for equality in the workplace against sexual harassment and discrimination, things she had endured from Harry for so long.

No, she would not let her mind wonder to Harry. She would not let her bitterness against him rule her days and nights. Over half her life was probably over, but she wasn't dead yet and she still had fight left in her. Yes, she would spend her days, from this day forth, helping women fight the good fight and these days there were certainly things to fight about. Maybe she would become a lawyer for Planned Parenthood. It was beyond outrageous that in 2015 in the year of our Lord, men continued to try and succeed in taking away women's rights concerning what went on in their own bodies. And those were the men who hated big government, except, of course, to insert that same big government into a woman's uterus. Suddenly Nora was very, very angry.

With her back to the street, as she continued digging and planting, she didn't see the ritzy sports car pull up and park in front of her house. A nervous looking Harry emerged from his car, saw Nora, took a deep breath and walked toward her.

Putting new shingles on the roof of the house next door, was a hard hat worker, or more specifically, the Goddess.

Now standing behind Nora, Harry called out her name.

Surprised, Nora whipped around on the ground. She managed to stand up, embarrassed at how she must look, muddy gloves on her hands, dirt on her face.

"What're you doing here, Harry?" she mustered.

"I thought we should talk, Nora."

Truth was, Harry was a complete and nervous wreck. Maybe she had a pistol, a real pistol this time, in the pocket of her overalls. It was now legal to carry firearms, real guns, pretty much anywhere, these days, thanks to the NRA and their influential money.

Nora pulled off her gloves, dropped them on the ground and stuck her hands into her pockets, which made Harry, immediately, take a few steps back.

"I don't think that's really appropriate, us talking, considering our day in court coming up." Nora said

"Nora, Nora," and there it was, that patronizing tone in Harry's voice. "I've moved passed all that. Hey, I didn't press charges for that ugly little scene of yours, did I?"

"What do you want, Harry?"

"Well, I thought, I just thought we could work something out, you know, just between the two of us."

"Oh, you mean now you're kissing up to me so I won't sue you for sexual discrimination?"

"Listen, Dear..." Harry started.

Nora gave him that 'Dear' look of hers.

"Listen, Nora, I've been thinking and well, how would you like to come back to the firm? We'd love to have you."

Nora couldn't help but laugh.

"Are you kidding me? Not even in another life."

Harry thought a moment and then another.

"Ah, Senior Partner! How 'bout that?"

"You could make me President and I'd never come back. You sound desperate, Harry, really desperate and it's not a pretty sight."

Harry was trying with all his might to keep his anger at bay. He was failing.

"Listen, I'm trying to be reasonable, here. I'm trying to make a deal with you!"

"Well, Harry, your dealing days with me are over."

Nora knew she now had the upper hand with him.

"Almost fifteen years ago, we made a deal, Harry, that if I stayed with you, you'd leave Emily and marry me. Some deal that was. How long did I wait for you? Five, six years?"

Reacting to this unbelievable and totally surprising news, the Goddess almost fell off the roof, next door. 'Who'd have figured that?' She thought.

"Oh, so that's what this is all about, huh? A woman scorned?" said Harry, not realizing that was a really, really stupid thing to say.

"Don't flatter yourself, Platt. I moved on from you years ago."

Nora then picked up a pair of large gardening shears that were on the ground and started working on some bushes.

Seeing the weapon, Harry backed away from her, again.

"So what, then? Did some shrink at that funny farm you were at suggest you do this, sue me, to get some, what do they call it these days, some closure or something?"

"Truth is, Harry, I should have done this to you years ago when I first deserved a partnership and you didn't give it to me. And why didn't you give it to me? Did you just think by stringing me along with empty promises, year after year, would keep me there? Promises to marry me. Promises for a partnership. But then, when you made Jeffrey Partner, well, that was my last straw. You passed me by for the last time!"

Nora continued chopping at the bushes. Chop. Chop. Chopping with her large shears.

"Listen, lady, you had nothing to complain about. I paid you big bucks. I taught you everything you know. You came to me out of law school, a novice. Where would you be without me?"

"Where would I be? I'd be getting big bucks at a company that respects me, that gives me my due for being one hell of a lawyer. That's where I'd be! But, no, I always stayed loyal to you, Harry, to you and to the firm. And for what?"

And it was at that moment that Harry knew there would be no negotiating with Nora.

"Good luck in court, then, Nora. You'll never win. You'll never win against me!"

Harry then turned away from her and quickly walked back to his car.

On the roof, the Goddess watched him drive away. 'I wouldn't bet my firm on it, if I were you, Harry,' She said to Herself.

Julie and Dick were taking a lovely walk in the park. Around them children were playing and families were having picnics on the grass. Wearing maternity clothes, Julie, now five months pregnant, looked lovely, fit and full of energy. Dick, on the other hand, was moving slowly.

"Can't we stop now and rest?" Dick whined. My back and legs are killing me."

He stopped walking, pulled up his pant legs and looked down.

"Oh wow, my ankles are so swollen," he continued to whine.

"C'mon, Dick, my doctor said that exercise was good for me and the baby."

"Oh, God. I feel like crap. I'm so queasy."

"Ya know, Dick, at first I thought it was sort of cute that you were having all my pregnancy symptoms, but enough, already," Julie told him.

"Well, thanks a million. I can't help the way I feel, Julie. You think I like feeling this way?"

"No, really. That first day I told you I was pregnant and you threw up and threw up and threw up…"

Dick was turning green, looking like he was going to barf on the spot.

"Stop saying that, Julie. I'm not kidding," moaned Dick.

"Ya know what, Dick? I thought it was because you didn't want a baby. But stop it, already! I'm the one having this baby and you're supposed to be taking care of me, not the other way around."

"I can't help the way I feel. And I'd appreciate just a little sympathy from you, that's all,"

"Well, for once why don't you think about how I feel? Where's any sympathy for me?" said Julie, now totally losing patience with her husband.

"Okay, okay. This feeling's gotta be over soon. I mean, you stopped being nauseous over a month ago."

A clown walked down the park path with a cart, selling cotton candy. It was the Goddess, of course.

"Hi, folks. How about a nice big cotton candy for your wife, Sir," the Goddess asked Dick.

She took one off Her cart and put it up to Dick's face. He caught a whiff and bolted. Ready to upchuck into a near-by trash can, he saw a park men's room and ran to it as fast as he could.

"Stomach flu? Be careful, Sweetie," the Goddess told Julie. "You don't want to get sick in your wonderful, beautiful condition."

136

"No, he's not sick. But it's just so weird. Since I've been pregnant, he's been having all the symptoms."

The Goddess smiled and gave her the cotton candy, gesturing that it was on the house, or the park, as the case was.

"As well it should be, don't you think?" the Goddess asks.

Julie didn't know quite how to respond.

The Goddess smiled again and went on Her way.

A few minutes later, Dick came out of the men's room, looking very pale. Holding his stomach, he walked over to where Julie was sitting on a bench, happily eating her cotton candy.

"Feeling better?" she asked him. "Want some, now?"

Dick looked at Julie, then at the cotton candy and again raced for the men's room.

On a city street filled with commercial buildings, Sally walked along, looking at the building's addresses. She checked the piece of paper she was holding, then up at the building in front of her. On the door was a plague that read, 'The House Of Romero.'

Sally straightened her short skirt, smoothed her hair and entered the building. She was quite nervous.

In the reception area of The House Of Romero, waiting for her name to be called, along with a few other women and men, she continually checked her watch. She then picked up a fashion magazine off the coffee table in front of her.

On the cover of the magazine was a picture of Tom with the article's title, "No More Morley.'

'I knew I made the right decision. I'm not going down with him,' she thought.

Finally, her name was called and a minute later she was sitting in an inner office, hoping to make a very good impression on Mr. Romero, himself, an extremely popular clothing designer.

And there Sally sat, waiting, fidgeting, waiting to be interviewed. Finally, a severe looking black woman, okay, the Goddess, entered the room and sat behind Her large desk.

"Sorry to keep you waiting. Your resume, please," said the Goddess, not in the friendliest tone Sally had ever heard.

Sally took out her resume from her briefcase, that also held her best ad work, and handed it over.

"I'm sorry, but I thought I would be meeting Mr. Romero," Sally said.

"Oh, no, he's much too busy for these preliminary interviews. I'm Ms. Amos. I, how do I say it, I screen out the undesirables."

And then She scanned Sally's resume.

"My, my, very impressive. You've worked for some of the best, haven't you?"

"Yes. I certainly have," said Sally, feeling somewhat more confident.

The Goddess continued to read.

"Oh... oh..." She said.

"What? Is something wrong," asked Sally.

"Tsk, tsk, tsk," said the Goddess.

'You know, I've won many awards for my ads..."

"Yes, I see. But what's this? Your last job was with..." and the Goddess leaned forward toward Sally and whispered, "Thomas Morley? Um, not good."

"But, but, I did some of my best work for him. I was with him almost five years. I helped him become who he is," Sally explained.

The Goddess looked long and hard at Sally and Sally quickly realized her mistake.

"Well, what I mean is, ah, well, of course, I could only work with what he gave me, in terms of his designs and, and *his* ideas, but..."

"Say no more," said the Goddess, smiling.

And at that, Sally looked relieved.

139

"Well, thank you for coming by," the Goddess said, standing up, ending the interview.

"But wait, that's it?" Sally asked, devastation engulfing her being.

"Well, yes. We couldn't think of hiring you... considering. You're unfortunately linked to his name, that is, what's left of it. Perhaps you should think of taking him off your resume."

"I can't do that! What'll I say I've been doing for the last five years? You know in this business you're only as good as your last ad!" said a desperate sounding Sally.

"Now, don't feel attacked, but need you say more? I'm sorry."

The Goddess handed Sally back her resume and walked out of the office.

Sally, quite paralyzed, just sat there, grief stricken.

"Shit!"

Tom was in his bed, tossing and turning. He was in the mist of a very bad dream.

This dream of his was in sepia tones. And there were eerie echoes everywhere.

Many women of all shapes and sizes were picketing in front of his building and they were chanting that familiar refrain, "Make Morley poorly. Make Morley poorly. Make Morley poorly." And the chanting went on and on.

And then, out of nowhere, a large black woman, seemingly floated onto the scene. She was wearing a dirty muu-muu and dusty hiking boots. A large spiral necklace hung around her neck. And she had wild and crazy hair.

"Come, my women. It is time," the large black woman said. "Come with me. It is time..."

And she started to lead all the women, of every size, of every color and age away.

Suddenly in his dream, as Tom continued tossing and turning in his bed, enveloped in this, his dream nightmare, the scene changed to a vast desert, with its rolling sand dunes, the sand stirred up by a constant wind. And walking across the dunes were all the women, including young girls and baby girls being carried by their mothers.

And leading all the women, young and old, girls and babies, was the large black woman. And they all seemed to glide across the sand in slow motion. And there, trying to follow them was Tom. He was ragged and oh, so tired.

"Wait... wait... Where are you going? Come back. Come back..." said the Tom in Tom's dream.

"It's too late... too late," said the large black woman.

"What do you mean, it's too late," asked the Tom in Tom's dream.

"It's too late. You don't respect us, any of us women," she answered.

"What do you mean? I respect you. I love women. I do…"

"No. And we have no nice clothes to wear. No nice clothes to wear. You don't make clothes for us. No nice clothes to wear…" she said "Come, my women. It is time. It is time to go…"

"You can't go. Come back. What will I do without women," Tom in Tom's dream asked, pleadingly.

"You should have thought of that before…"

"But when will you be back," he asked.

"Never… never… never…," the large black woman told him.

And then her voice faded away, as did all the women, large and small, young and old.

The desert sands stopped blowing and what was left was… nothing. Nothing but a world without women.

In his sleep, Tom moaned a loud moan.

"Come back… You can't go. Please come back. What can I do? Please don't go…" Tom mumbled in his turbulent state of sleep.

And then he suddenly awoke from his nightmare. He sat up in his bed, shaken and sweating.

"What the hell…?"

On the line between Heaven and Earth God was standing on his tippy-toes, trying to get in the Goddess's face. He failed.

"Whatta ya doing, for God's… for… my sake? Huh?!" God was low on energy, but high on anger.

"Well, whatever do you mean?" replied the Goddess, innocently.

"You're still messing with my people! Stop it, stop it, stop it!!"

"What are you talking about? They are simply exercising their free will, that which you gave them, remember?"

"Free will, my backside! You're trying to change them! You're, you're putting them into situations they would have never thought of being in."

God had, actually, not thought of saying this to Her, but Ted had prepped him on how to deal with Her.

"Oh, my… and I wonder why that would be, that they would never have thought to… what? I do believe your rules are quite possibly changing. Options, Pops! The way I figure it, they've… and I'm talking women, here, have been living all these years thinking they've had no other options but the status quo. *Your* status quo. Yes, the status is a changin'. Change is good, right?"

"No! It's not! I don't like change! I like things just the way they've always been."

"Oh, yes, so did I. So did I, until you came along and..."

"...Oy, please, please, please, let's not start that again," he interrupted Her. "It's ancient history." And then He had a long coughing attack.

"So it is. Ah, but I remember it well. I remember when I was respected and revered and loved, just like you are, now. And women were revered, too. Ah, yes, the days of me, the Great Mother, the good old days. There was peace and harmony and love," She said dreamily, getting teary eyed, remembering.

God, God hated to see Her cry.

"Now, now, now, my Dear. You keep dwelling on the negative. You're still important. I keep telling you that. Look at all the lovely things you continue to do. The plants and flowers and the trees. And what about all the little furry animals? And the big furry animals, too. Wondrous, really wondrous."

"Oh, who are you kidding, Daddy-O?!" The Goddess was angry, again. "They're cutting down my forests and hunting some of my best animals. They're sucking me dry with all their drilling. Oil is spilling out over my land and seas, my world is polluted and you wonder why I can't get the sun up on time?!"

"Well, hey, you're not blaming me for all that, are you?"

"Oh, no, it's never your fault. It's *their* fault, right? But who do they listen to? Who do they pray to for guidance? Who do they use as an excuse for everything? Well, now they're going to listen to ME!! It's time for them to listen to their Mother, again!!"

And at that, the Goddess stormed off, leaving Him standing alone, shaking his throbbing head and very, very worried.

"Oy vey, what is She gonna do next?" said a very, very dizzy God.

CHAPTER TWELVE

<u>WHAT SHE DOES NEXT</u>

The hallway outside of the courtroom was crowded with people milling around, waiting for court to commence. Among the milling people was Harry. By his side, hanging on his every word and his arm, as well, was his, still adoring, wife, Emily. Talking with them was Jeffrey.

A few feet away and standing alone, was Nora. Harry looked over and zinged out a dirty look to her. She saw the zinger, but her face didn't respond in any way. She just stood there, pretending she hadn't seen or felt it.

"Now, Harry, don't worry about anything. I've done my homework. There won't be any surprises. Believe me, it's in the bag," Jeffrey said with confidence.

"I hope you're right. Oh God, I hope you're right, Jeffrey."

"Not to worry, my Dear," Emily told her husband. "It'll turn out just fine. I still just can't believe Nora would try and do something else to you. I wonder what made her become such an angry, hostile, nasty person?"

"Me neither, my Dear. Me neither," said loving hubby Harry.

He, again, glanced Nora's way.

"I swear, I swear to God, I still just don't understand what I could have possibly done to make her this angry," Harry said to his wife, knowing full well he did.

"Well, my Darling, considering her behavior, trying to shoot you and now this, you made the right decision not to make her Partner. You and the firm have a reputation to uphold. It's so clear to me that she's totally unstable. She could have ruined everything you've spent your life working for," Emily told Harry, stroking his back with her gloved hand.

The doors of the courtroom opened and everyone began to file in. Within minutes, every seat in the large room was filled. This case had gotten gobs of publicity that brought out regular court watchers, feminist groups, male lawyers interested in how the jury would rule on this sex discrimination case and of course, the media.

Harry, his little group and Nora got to the door of the courtroom at the same time. A moment passed to see who would enter first. Just as Nora thought Harry would yield to her, he pushed by her and led Emily through the door. As Emily passed Nora, she gave her the evil eye, something Emily was quite good at doing to those she wasn't fond of, disliked intensely, was jealous of, or to folks she believed to be beneath her on a social level.

Finally, Nora passed into the room of justice, talking a very deep breath as she went in.

It took a little while for everyone to get seated. Harry and Jeffrey sat down at the defense table, with Emily sitting right behind her husband. At the plaintiff's table, Nora sat alone. Jeffrey looked around the room, then at the door to see if anyone else was coming in, then to Nora.

"Looks like she's defending herself, Harry," he said.

"Well, maybe that's better for us. As good as she is, she'll probably get all emotional and out of control and it'll be no contest," said Harry, trying to think positive.

Emily leaned forward, kissed Harry on the back of his neck and whispered to him, "Are you alright, Darling? You'll see, everything will turn out fine. I'm sure of it. Justice will be done."

Harry nodded, but said nothing. He was nervous. Very, very nervous.

And as far as nervousness went, so was Nora, as she looked around the room.

Finally, the Bailiff came out and told everyone to rise. Everyone rose.

The door to the Judge's chambers opened and someone in the courtroom was heard saying, "Here comes the Judge. Here comes the Judge!"

And there she came. She was very short and her Judge's robe looked to be a size too big for her, with the robe sleeves going well past her teeny hands, the hem way past her minute feet. She almost tripped walking to her large chair in front of the courtroom. When she finally sat down, because of her petite size and the largeness of the chair, she all but disappeared behind her huge desk. At the sight of this, there were immediate titters and muffled giggles from the court watchers.

If one was to believe any of this disturbed or distracted Judge Sophie, they'd be wrong.

"Hey, Sonny!" Sophie called out to the Bailiff.

Knowingly, he picked up two phone books from under his own table and rushed them over to her. She stood up as he placed the books under her, then he lifted her up to sit down on them. Through all of this, she held her head high with dignity.

"Thank you. Much better," she told the Bailiff. "Alrighty, court is in session! Let's see, what'd we have on the docket, today?"

Sophie looked over a bunch of papers on her desk.

"Oh, yes, yes, yes. A sexual discrimination suit. Better that then a Gabardine suit!"

The courtroom filled with laughter and Sophie was quite happy with their reaction and herself, for that matter.

"Okay, sorry. Just bringing a little levity to a very serious problem, which seems to run rampant in our society today," Sophie stated.

Harry and Jeffrey couldn't believe this judge and her prejudicial statement.

"Okay, okay, so, who's representing who... I mean whom?"

As if perfect in its timing, the courtroom doors burst open and down the aisle strutted Nora's attorney. Of course, it was the Goddess. She was dressed in authentic African garb, a long, colorful caftan-type dress and a matching turban-type headdress. Without a doubt, She was a dramatic sight to behold.

Seeing Her, Nora breathed a sign of relief, as the Goddess sat down next to her.

"Well, Helloooo," Judge Sophie said, greeting this wonderfully dressed lawyer, in her opinion.

"So sorry I'm late, Your Honor," said the Goddess, smiling at Sophie.

Although since She was facing Sophie, no one caught the wink She also gave her.

"No, no, you haven't missed anything. The fun hasn't yet begun."

"Why do I have the distinct feeling we're already in big trouble?" Harry asked Jeffrey, sheer apprehension in his voice.

"We're fine, Harry, don't worry," was Jeffrey's answer, although not exactly what the young lawyer/Partner was feeling at that moment.

"Please! Hushness in the courtroom," demanded Sophie, hearing Jeffrey and Harry whispering to each other.

"So, okie-dokie," she continued. "I see a Jeffrey Harkness is the attorney for Harry Platt and Kali Ma Shapiro is the plaintiff's lawyer. What an interesting name you have, Ms. Shapiro."

"I don't believe this," Harry whispered to Jeffrey.

"Well, Your Honor, my father was Jewish, hence the Shapiro, obviously, and Kali Ma is from my mother's side. It means dark and time," the Goddess told the court.

"Hmm, how very interesting. Tell me more."

At this, Harry socked Jeffrey in the ribs, motioning for him to object. Jeffrey did what he was told.

"Your Honor, I don't understand what's going on. We haven't...'

"Hush! Sit! I'm workin' here," Sophie admonished Jeffrey.

Jeffrey sat.

"So, go on, Ms. Shapiro, or is it Ms. Ma Shapiro?" Sophie chortled to herself.

The Goddess stood up, looking quite imposing, especially to Her opposition.

"Kali Ma was a Hindu Goddess. An aspect of the Mother from whom all are born and to whom all must return. She created, but She also destroyed!"

The Goddess's last words were directed straight at Harry. Seeing this, he cowered a bit.

"Well, what a bit of history, or in this case, I guess it's *Her* story."

Judge Sophie was really getting a kick out of herself.

"Could we please get on with the trial, Your Honor?" asked the impatient Jeffrey.

"Right you are! Ms. Abrams, call your first witness.

"Yes, I call Susan Peters to the stand."

Once the lovely Susan Peters took the stand and some questioning, the Goddess asked of her, "And you did not get the promised promotion?"

"No. I waited two years to be Mr. Platt's clerk, but every time, a man was given the job, the job that should have been, by all rights, mine," answered Susan.

What ensued was the Goddess calling woman witness after woman witness, questioning them and getting answers back.

"And in these years were you ever given your deserved raise?"

'No. No promotion. No raise. And he promised them to me," answered Gloria.

"And who was it who got the raise and promotion instead of you?"

'The son of a friend of Mr. Platt's," answered Maryann.

"And at that time, had he promised you a Junior Partnership?"

"That's right. He promised me," answered Carla.

"He promised me," answered Linda

"He promised me," answered Suzanne.

"He promised me. The things I did for that man to be an Associate in his firm," answered Jane.

The Goddess looked hard at Jane.

"Really? Exactly what kind of things?"

"Listen, I knew what the competition was out there to work for Harry Platt in that capacity. He is a great lawyer," continued Jane.

"What exactly are you saying, Jane?" inquired the Goddess innocently.

"I'm saying, I needed an edge."

"And dare I ask what exactly that edge was?"

And then Jane started to cry.

"Let's just say I made sure to be... available to him," Jane said between sobs.

"Well, let's just say you *slept* with him! Isn't that true?" asked the Goddess, Her voice with an accusatory tone, as She turned to look Harry straight in the eye.

"Yes, I slept with him," answered Renee.

"I slept with him," answered Andrea.

"I slept with him, too." answered Barbara 'I know I shouldn't have, but I did. And what did it get me? Nothing!"

Listening to each of these women testify, Emily reacted with horror, first not believing, knowing in her heart these women were lying, lying, lying, but there were so many of them. So many.

"Liar! Liar!! They're all liars!!" screamed Harry, completely out of order.

"Harry! Sit down!" ordered Jeffrey to his client.

Judge Sophie banged her mega, mega gavel, one the same size John Boehner got when he took over as Speaker Of The House.

"Order in the court! Order in the court! Gee, I love saying that," said Sophie, giddy with power. "Okay, you may continue, Ms. Shapiro."

"Thank you, Judge. And after you slept with him, did you get your promotion?"

"No, he fired me," said Kathy.

"He fired me," said Sherri.

"He fired me," said Betty.

"Of course I wasn't promoted. He had his way with me and then I was given the boot!" said Diane.

"No more questions," said the Goddess.

Harry turned to Emily for comfort, but she had none to give him. Instead, she got up and ran from the room, hysterically crying.

"Emily! Emily, Dear! Wait! Wait," Harry yelled. "They're all lying bitches," he said, too loudly, as he raced up the courtroom aisle after her.

There was a collective gasp from all the court watchers, as those in the media, hurriedly scribbled down notes on their pads.

"Your Honor, I rest my case," the Goddess proudly said.

"Well, from what I've just heard, I think it's Mr. Platt who needs a rest."

Laughter was heard throughout the courtroom, as the Goddess went back to Her seat next to Nora. They then, 'high-fived' each other.

A deal was later made and Nora knew she would be able to live quite comfortably for the rest of her life, that her garden would always be filled with blooming flowers.

Ted hadn't been able to keep his eyes off of the gripping court drama that had just ended on the TV monitor in his office. In comparison, God was slumped in a chair with a large bag of ice on his aching head.

"I'm cold, Ted. I'm so cold," God told Ted, His teeth chattering.

Ted turned off the monitor, then removed the ice pack from God's head. He then grabbed a blanket from his executive assistant closet and tucked it around his boss. Within five minutes God complained how hot he was. Then he sneezed twice.

For the next half an hour, God alternated between the ice on his head and the blanket around his body.

"That, that was a complete and utter travesty of justice!" Ted told God.

"I thought She looked quite swell in that get-up, didn't you?" said God, His words slurring together a tad..

"I'm not talking about how She looked, I'm talking about the case. I betya She and that idiotic Judge Sophie paid all those women to testify! And why didn't Jeffrey object, object, object! I've seen better lawyering on Ally McBeal, for God's sake!"

"Are you using my name in vain, you young… young… whippersnapper?"

It was obvious that God might have been running a fever and was somewhat delirious. On the other hand, it might have been the strong decongestant Ted had given Him for his cold.

"And does that twit servant of Her's even have a degree in judging? How did they do that? How is She doing everything She's doing? How, how, how?!"

"Oy, enough, Ted. Can't you see I'm under the weather? Under the weather. She makes the weather and I'm… under Her, then." And God started giggling.

And Ted was losing patience with Him.

"Supreme Father of Everything, I think it's beddy-bye time for you."

"Really?" said God feeling very, very woozy. "O-kay, but I need my teddy bear to fall asleep."

"Fine, I'll get your teddy bear. Now, c'mon..."

Ted, literally, had to pick God up and carry him to His bedroom.

The minute he got back to his office, he once again turned on his monitors to see what in God's name She was up to, now. No, whatever She was up to, it was certainly not in God's name.

In Dick and Julie's living room, Dick was watching an old, black and white episode of Perry Mason. Lying on the couch, he looked like he was going to cry.

Julie, quite pregnant, now, came into the room, from the kitchen, with pizza and soft drinks on a tray. She looked glowingly healthy and more lovely than ever. She looked at her near tears husband.

"What's the matter, now, Dick?"

"I don't think he's going to solve this case. I just don't," Dick said in a very weepy voice.

Julie put the tray of food down on the coffee table, then sat down on the couch, beside him.

"Ah, don't worry, Sweetheart, Perry always finds a way, you know that," she said sarcastically. "C'mon now, eat your pizza."

Dick took a piece and gobbled it up in one big bite.

"Do ya think he really will solve the case?" he garbled, his mouth still pizza-filled.

"Yes, yes, Dear, I think."

Julie watched Dick pig out and rolled her eyes.

"Well, at least it's good to see you finally got your appetite back."

"Are you making fun of me?" Dick said, all weepy, again.

"I'm not making fun of you," she told him, sighing.

"You know I've been eating fine once we got to the end of the second trimester," he reminded her.

"Yes, you're right, Dick. You're right."

"Well, when you criticize my eating habits, it just makes me feel really bad, that's all, Julie."

"I'm sorry," Julie said, rolling her eyes again.

"You don't think I've gained weight, do you?" Dick said, now outright crying.

"No, Dick, you haven't gained weight, well, just a little, but I have to say, I think I liked you better when you were throwing up."

"Ya know, Jules, that's not even funny. But you actually think I've gained weight?"

Julie had finally lost patience with him. "Dick! Hello! How many times do I have to tell you, this is *my* pregnancy. It's not about you! It's about me and the baby. For eight months now, you've made everything about you and I'm tired of it."

"I'm sorry. I know it is. Really, I do. Do you think you could rub my lower back? It's killing me," he complained.

Julie could only shake her head.

"Oh, sure. Where does it hurt? Actually, maybe I'm lucky you're this way now, instead of that football loving macho guy you used to be."

He looked at her with a very hurt expression. She started rubbing his back and he moaned, happily. Then he laid his head down on Julie's swollen belly.

Back in Ted's office, he too was watching the Perry Mason episode.

"Oh, for God's sake, it's not him! It's the other guy! C'mon, Perry, nail him!"

Just then, God stumbled into the room.

"Where am I? What time is it? Where am I?"

"Sir? Sir? Are you alright? Couldn't you sleep?" asked Ted., now quite worried about God.

"I don't feel so good. Did you put something in my tea?"

"No, I just gave you something for your sniffle."

"I have a sniffle?" And just then God sneezed four times in a row.

"I think you must rest, All Powerful Person. The way things are going down there, I think you'll need all your strength. Everything seems to be going upside down."

"Upside down. Round and round," God started singing.

"Okay, that's it, Sir. I think I'll get that Doctor Kevorkian in to see you. He's supposed to be very good. I'm sure he'll be able to have you alive and kicking again, soon."

CHAPTER THIRTEEN

EAT, PRAY, LOVE

Sally had become quite depressed trying to find work and that was an understatement. She was also angry and quite frankly, pissed off. No matter how impressed fashion houses were with her work, it always came down to the years she had worked for Tom. No one would touch her with a ten foot pole. But she still had not taken her time with him off her resume, for then, how could she possibly account for those five years? She was also starting to feel extremely nervous, since her bank account, once filled with the green stuff, was quickly dwindling.

Finally, she knew she had no choice, not to mention she was running out of fashion houses to interview with. Of course, she had also tried to find work at any advertising agencies in town, but they, too, of course knew about her fall from grace and wouldn't touch her with a ten foot pole, either, much less a twenty foot pole.

At the appointed hour, Sally found herself sitting across from her interviewer's desk, knowing if she didn't get a job, there, well, what the hell would she do, then? Everything, her life, her mind, her self worth, everything was riding on this interview with one Ms. Matilda Fox of the Jonas Bean Fashion House. Jonas Bean wasn't what one could call 'high fashion,' rather he did knock-offs of famous designer's clothes, then tailored them to the younger set. Teens. Of course, it was a complete come down for Sally, but she was desperate.

"I started out working for Rush Designs, right out of art school and won Best Print Ad Award my first year there. And remember when Amour Fashions came out with their very short, very skimpy, very sexy line? Well, their 'Less With Amour' slogan was mine! I'm good, Ms. Fox. I'm very good!"

Did Ms. Matilda Fox detect desperation in Sally's voice? Yes she did and considering

Matilda was really Sophie, she was thoroughly enjoying herself.

"Well, well, Sally, this is all very, very impressive."

Sally smiled, just feeling in her gut that she, momentarily, would be employed.

"Thank you. And you'll never find a harder worker, a more innovated worker than me! And I work really well with people I work with. I'm absolutely a 'There is no 'I' in team, kinda person!"

"Certainly good to hear, but I just have one little question. What have you been doing for the last five years?" asked Matilda/Sophie, innocently, waiting with baited breath for Sally's answer or lie, as, no doubt, would be the case.

'Damn,' thought Sally. The dreaded question. She had come up with all kinds of scenarios, just in case the question was asked, but her favorite that had come to her after drinking too much red wine, one night, that of being kidnapped and put into a Mexican jail for years, just didn't seem a plausible concept anyone would believe.

Sophie was tapping a pencil on her desk, waiting for an answer.

"Well, ah, well, see… ah, I…"

"It's alright, Dearie. Did the pressure of the business finally get you down and you just took a little break? Actually, a long break, in your case. Is that what happened? You can tell me."

"Well, yes, sort of..." Sally said in an almost whisper.

"Yes, yes, I can certainly understand. We all have to sometimes take a break, regain our strength, our power, so that we can again go out there and make change, make a difference!" Sophie was sure she was sounding incredibly profound.

"Yes! That's what happened! And now I'm back, rested and ready to make a difference, hopefully by working for Jonas Bean Fashions!" For the first time in months, Sally was again feeling confident.

"Yes, knowing when you need to take a break and doing it is wonderful and certainly better than doing something horrible, like working for someone like, say... that vile loser, Thomas Morley and not wanting to admit it! Right?"

At that moment, Sally knew the jig was up. Ms. Asshole Fox had known the whole time about her.

Her face redder than red, Sally bolted for the door, slamming it behind her.

"Well, gee, was it something I said?" chuckled Sophie.

Sally ran out of the Jonas Bean building. She was hysterically crying and she continued to cry as she ran down the street, having no direction, knowing not where she was heading.

She ran and ran until she could run no more, finding herself in front of a pizza parlor. She dried her tears as she looked in the window at all the people inside, looking so happy, stuffing their faces with the tasty delight.

She entered the establishment, ordered herself an extra large pizza with a side of spaghetti and a bunch of garlic bread and ingested it all in quick order.

After interviewing with a local community free paper and not getting the job, Sally ate two hot fudge sundaes. After not getting two jobs as secretaries, she ate an entire cherry pie, then a chocolate cake, all in one sitting. After being turned down for a job at a Gap store, she ate three long Subway sandwiches. After not getting a job as a waitress at an Olive Garden, she sat down in one of their booths and ate half their menu. After losing a shoe renting job at a bowling ally, she gorged herself on lots and lots of Chinese food.

And so it went for Sally and soon she no longer looked like one of those skinny models in high fashion clothes she used to make up ads for. No, now Sally was very, very fat.

One night, after taking a shower, she dropped her towel and for the first time in a very, very long time, really looked at herself in the mirror. Seeing her massive refection, she started to weep.

"Oh, God, what's become of me?"

Tom was also depressed, although he was hardly eating, at all. The poor guy couldn't get arrested and was scorned by anyone who happened to recognize him on the street. And so, he started going out in disguises. Nothing outrageous, just a baseball cap pulled down low on his forehead, big sunglasses and jeans and tennies, instead of his usual designer duds.

Most of the time he spent alone in his office, trying to come up with new and fabulous designs, a sensational and different kind of clothing line, something that would bring his once sparkling reputation back from the dead. As it was, he had lost almost all of his investors and if he didn't think of something fast, a big comeback, he would lose his prestigious offices. Duane was still with him, although Tom didn't know how much longer he'd be able to pay him.

When one was flying high, living the life, one tended not to think about what happened if it were all to disappear, something Tom was now living. Everything he had worked so hard for had, in fact, disappeared. And he was one depressed puppy.

One day he found himself walking aimlessly around a street flea market which was crowded with people shopping for bargains. He knew there would be nothing there he could use for inspiration, that was for sure, not that he didn't pray day and night to God for something to stimulate his creative mind.

A heavy set African woman was at her booth, selling perfume. It was *not* the Goddess. As Tom walked by, she held up a bottle of her perfume, a bottle in the shape of the Goddess icon, found in the earth all those eons ago, with Her rounded hips and large breasts.

"You want to smell? It is very, very good. Very sensual," the African woman told him.

Not wanting to be rude, Tom put the bottle up to his nose and breathed in.

"Mm… interesting," he said.

"You want to buy? Only I have this scent. African Musk. It is very, very special smell, aye? You want to buy?" she pressed him.

"No, thank you, not today," he told her.

"Well, you know where to find me. Here every weekend. You be back. Yes."

Tom smiled at her and went on his way.

A few feet away, another booth was filled with beautiful Batik fabrics. Tom looked through the fabrics, touching them, holding them up to the sunlight. Then he put them down and continued on his way.

And he wondered, still, where was the inspiration he was looking for?

Harry was sitting in his large, opulently decorated bedroom, in his large chair, staring out the window as the sun set in the west. He was very, very depressed. The phone on his bed stand rang and he almost didn't answer it. But he did.

"Hello... Doctor Berman wants me to come in, again? ...Okay, fine, Thursday, eleven o'clock. I'll be there."

Harry hung up the phone, as a chill suddenly went through his entire body. He started unbuttoning his shirt, thinking he'd take a hot bath, have a glass of his favorite white wine and go to bed early.

He walked into his massive walk-in closet and turned on the light. It was filled with his many pairs of expensive shoes, all lined up neatly on shelves. His sweaters were all perfectly folded on more open shelves. His pants and jackets hung on hangers that were exactly two inches apart from each other.

And then Harry glanced at the other side of the huge closet. It was empty. And Harry, yearningly, looked at the empty racks and shelves where Emily's clothes and purses and shoes once were housed. Yes, she had left him after finding out the truth of his life in court and there wasn't a trace of her left in his big mansion. Not a trace.

Off a hook on the closet door Harry took down his monogrammed bathrobe and slowly went into his huge marble bathroom, hoping to soak his troubles away.

In front of the building that housed Thomas Morley Fashions, no women walked around chanting 'Make Morley poorly,' since they had pretty much succeeded in doing that.

Sally, fat Sally, wearing sunglasses, a scarf covering her head and a big coat wrapped around her heft, even though it was quite warm outside, walked up to the building she knew so well. On the directory where companies housed inside were listed, was a small sign that read: Thomas Morley Fashions, 23rd Floor, Temporarily Closed.

Sally read it, then sadly walked away.

In a gynecologist's office in a medical building, sat Julie and Dick, waiting. A few minutes later, Doctor Lilith Hardy swept in. She was wearing a white lab coat and a stethoscope hung around Her neck. She sat down at her desk and looked at Dick and Julie. Of course, it was really the Goddess.

"Morning, Julie. And how are you feeling?"

"Fine, Doctor. Getting anxious, though."

"Of course, you are. Not that much longer before you bring new life into this world. Very exciting. And you must be Dick."

The truth was, She had never met Dick before. Since he hated all doctors, he hadn't felt it necessary to go with Julie to her appointments, much to Julie's chagrin.

"Julie tells me you've had some bad months," the Goddess said, smiling.

"Oh, I have, Doc. I threw-up the first five months. Then I started getting these terrible leg cramps. And oh, my back's been killing me. But the worst are the mood swings. I get so weepy. Honestly, like I'll be watching reruns of Seinfeld and for no reason, no reason at all, I'll just burst into tears. Is that normal? Julie says it is, but I don't think that it is," he blabbed away.

"Well, yes it is… for *Julie*!!"

"But I just can't control it. Isn't there something you could give me for it?" he said, starting to weep.

"See, Doctor Hardy, I told you. It's like I already have a baby, before I even have a baby," said Julie, shaking her pretty head.

"Well, don't worry. Sometimes husbands do feel this way during their wife's pregnancy, only usually not to this extent. Dick, have you told your regular doctor about all your symptoms?" She asked.

"Yeah, I did and can you believe he told me I should go on Prozac?! I mean, Prozac, in my condition?!' said Dick, wiping his eyes.

It was no surprise what a kick the Goddess was getting from listening to Dick.

"Well, let's go into the examining room and have a look at who's causing all this trouble."

Dick immediately stood up and started to go into the exam room.

"Thank you, Doctor, thank you so much," said Dick

Julie looked up at him, then awkwardly tried to rise for... two.

A few minutes later, Julie was lying on the table, having an ultra-sound. On the screen was Julie's womb, inside of which was the image of her baby.

Dick stood right up to the screen, amazed, looking at the grainy image.

"Wow! Wow! Oh wow! That's my baby! Do you see it?! That's my baby! Look, Julie!" said a very excited Dick.

"If you'd move, Dick, maybe I could!"

Dick didn't move, totally mesmerized by what he was looking at.

Finally the Goddess, literally pushed him aside so Julie could see the screen.

"Aww... it's so much bigger than last time," exclaimed Julie, happily.

"Our baby, Julie. Our little boo-boo,' he was again weepy. "Can you tell what it is, Doc? Boy or girl?"

The Goddess studied the screen, then winked at Julie.

"No, sorry. From the position it's in, it's impossible to tell," She told him.

"I told you, I didn't want to know, Dick. I want to be surprised," Julie told her husband.

"Right. Right. Just as long as it's healthy, right? It's healthy, right, Doc?"

"Looks to be just fine and dandy to me," the Goddess told him. "Now, Dick, if you could just leave for a moment while I examine Julie."

"Aw, do I have to?"

"Dick!!" said an embarrassed Julie.

"Don't worry, Dick, when the big day comes, we won't leave you out. I'm expecting you in the delivery room to help Julie with her labor and to cut the cord!"

The realization of what was ahead for him hit Dick and he doubled over in pain, held his mouth and ran for the door, then out of the room.

"Dick? Dick, are you okay?" Julie called after him.

"Oh, men! I can't wait for him to experience labor pains," laughed the Goddess.

The Goddess then helped Julie put her feet into the stirrups.

In another examining room, in another part of the medical building, another set of feet were in stirrups. They were Harry's.

Standing next to the sheet-draped Harry was his doctor, Ronald Berman.

"Harry, I showed your test results to a specialist in the field," Doctor Berman told Harry.

"I'm scared, Doc."

"Best in the business, Harry. You'll be in good hands."

Just then, the exam room opened and in walked the Goddess, still as Doctor Lilith Hardy.

"Wonderful, Lilith. Right on time."

"I always am, Ronald," She happily said. "I always am."

Harry bolted up, the sheet covering him, almost falling off.

"Wait a minute! A woman doctor? For me?! For this?! For... *there*?!" Harry was quite close to being hysterical, not to mention being spread-eagle on the table.

"Calm down, Harry. Doctor Hardy has done ground-breaking work in this area. She actually switched to OB-GYN, but she's doing this, seeing you, as a special, personal favor to me, because you're such a close friend."

"Hello, Harry. Now, don't be afraid. I'm only here to help you. Believe me," said the Goddess.

"I'll talk with you after you examine him, Lilith," Doctor Berman said, before leaving the room.

The Goddess nodded to him, then approached the end of the examining table to take a good look at what was in between Harry's hairy legs.

After a few agonizing minutes, for Harry, that is, the Goddess emerged from under the sheet, leaving Harry's legs in the stirrups.

"Well, Harry, the x-rays and my exam confirm it. I'm afraid you have cancer of the testicles."

Harry's worst nightmare was confirmed. He wanted to ask a million questions, but this news had rendered him mute.

"Now, I know this isn't the news you were hoping for, but the good part is, I think we've caught it in time. I don't believe it's life-threatening, if we act quickly," She continued.

"So... so... so, what are you going to do to me?" he asked trembling in fear.

"Well, I'm going to *dig* in there and take out that nasty tumor, that's what I'm going to do!"

"That's it? Then I'll be fine?" said an only somewhat relieved Harry.

"Well, we hope you'll be fine. You might need some chemo and radiation. But truthfully, Harry, there's only one way to insure a complete and healthy recovery."

"What? What's that? I'll do it1 I'll do whatever it takes! I don't want to die!"

"Well, we cut 'em off!" the Goddess told him, matter-of-factly.

"I wanna die!!" cried Harry.

"Now, now, Harry, calm down a minute. Be sensible. You aren't intending to have any children, not at your age, are you?" asked the Goddess.

"No. I guess not."

"Well, the fact is, Harry, you just don't need them, anymore. Their usefulness is over. Done. Fini. Kaput. I say, get rid of them!"

"I wanna die..." Harry said, as he looked at Her in a panicked, pleading manner.

CHAPTER FOURTEEN

<u>GETTIN' DOWN WITH HER BAD SELF</u>

Having just watched this scene play itself out, Ted and God sat, cringing, in front of the TV monitor, both holding their own crotches.

"Okay, that's it!" said an incensed Ted. "Now She's gone too far!"

"Oy, I don't feel so good," said God. And He coughed up a bunch of phlegm, which he spit into the spittoon, next to him, that Ted had thoughtfully brought into his office.

God was bundled up, wearing earmuffs over his skull cap and a long, white scarf, wrapped three times around his neck, that Ted had knitted for him.

"She must be stopped, Your Godliness and now!"

"But what to do?" asked God, who was having a coughing fit. "If only I felt stronger."

"Sir, I think She's the culprit. I think somehow, She has zapped all your energy, Your Powerfulness. Yes, that must be it!" Ted said emphatically.

"Ya think?"

And then Ted thought and thought and thought.

"Or... maybe She's really the Devil, in disguise! Do you think She could do that? Take over his body, like that? Or *he* could?"

"Could what, Teddy?"

"Pretend to be *Her*? Yes, maybe that's it!" Ted's eyes were darting all around his head, trying to figure out what the hell was happening. "Maybe the Devil has taken over *Her* body and is making all this mayhem down there!"

And then Ted thought some more. And some more.

"Naw, that can't be it. It's not the devil's M.O. Although, I have seen him sit on folk's shoulders telling them to do very bad things. Whatta you think, Boss?"

"I think it's time for my meds," said God, His face flushed with fever.

Ted totally ignored Him and clicked his TV remote to another station to see what in the world She (or was it he?), might be up to, now. And then Ted wondered if he should risk going 'way down there' and ask the Devil, himself. No! The last time he tried that, his white wings and halo had gotten completely singed, not to mention, he was almost torched to death from the burning fires of hell. And that three-headed dog wasn't the friendliest of pets.

By this time, God had dozed off and was dreaming of soaking in one of the Goddess's marvelous hot springs.

As it happened, inspiration had, in fact, come to Tom. He wasn't sure it had any commercial possibilities, but a very strong sense of creativity had enveloped his heart and soul and so he decided to go with it. Anyway, at that point, he had nothing to lose.

A large, colorful sign had been posted on the door of Tom's show rehearsal room stating: OPEN CALL FOR MODELS FOR THE NEW LINE OF THOMAS MORLEY FASHIONS, TODAY, 11 AM.

The room had a small stage with a short runway. Chairs were set up for those models auditioning. On the stage, there was a large backdrop, a huge painting of a desert with rolling sand dunes, all in warm, earthy hues. Beautiful batik fabrics, like the ones Tom had seen at the flea market, hung from the stage. Also set up on easels, on the stage, were large sketches of thin, female manikins, wearing modern, yet ethnic type designs.

Eight or nine models milled around, some sitting on the chairs, waiting for the audition to begin. Tom, sitting at a small desk near the stage looked around, already disappointed at the low turnout.

Duane, Tom's long time assistant, sat at a table near the door, checking models in. Two thin, beautiful, of course, white models walked up to Duane.

"Well, hello! Welcome to Thomas Morley Fashions. Your name is…?"

"Tiffany Blaine," said the first girl.

"Pictures?" Duane asked for.

Tiffany handed him her professional photos.

"Very nice. Here's you number," he said handing her a numbered card.

Then he did the same to the next girl, Taylor Cates.

"Fabulous. We'll be starting momentarily, so if you'll please just have a seat, we'll be calling your number soon," Duane told them.

"There sure isn't anyone here," Taylor said to her friend, Tiffany. "I knew this was a mistake. Everyone says Thomas Morley will never make a comeback."

"Hush your mouth, girl," Duane told her. "Shame on you! Mr. Morley is coming back, bigger than ever!"

"Well, I'm not sure I even want to be associated with him, now."

Taylor thought for a moment, then took her photo back from Duane and left.

"Your loss, Honey," Duane called after her. "And what about you... Tiffany? Are you leaving, too?"

"No. I'll stay."

Duane smiled at her and pointed for her to take a seat.

A few more girls, but not many, enter the room and were checked in by Duane.

Tom looked at his watch and knew it was now or never, no matter how few models were there. He also knew he only needed one perfect one to be the face and body for his new line. And so he went up onto the stage, to a light smattering of applause.

"Thank you all for coming. I'm Thomas Morley and I know you all must be aware of the, well, I'll just say it, the boycotting of my company during this past year. And yes, it's been hard for me, but now I hope to make a comeback with my new line of clothing, that I believe in my heart, even my detractors will like. So, let's get started. Number One to the stage, please."

Tom went back to his desk and turned on a fan, which made the batik fabrics on the stage begin to gently blow, as if being in a soft wind.

Duane went to Tom's desk, handing him all the models photos and corresponding numbers. Tom then slipped a CD into the player and the music began.

The first model began to strut her stuff, smiling at Tom as she walked down the short runway. As she modeled, Tom took notes.

And so it went, model after model. In Tom's estimation, there were definitely some real possibilities in front of him.

Then, suddenly, there was some kind of commotion at Duane's table, near the room's door. Tom tried to ignore it, instead, keeping his eye on those he thought would be his prize.

"I'm sorry, Ma'am, but you must be mistaken," Duane told the woman who seemed to be the culprit of the commotion.

"But on the door it says 'Open Call For Models.'"

"Yes, it does, but oh, pu-leaze, you're definitely *not* a model."

"Well, excuse me, but yes, I am!"

"Whatever! Sorry, but you're all wrong for us! All wrong! Now, let's just not make a scene and go away. Go on, go away!" and he made a 'shooing' gesture with his graceful hands.

The woman Duane was talking to was dressed in ethnic garb, not that unlike the batik fabrics hanging on the stage. Must it be mentioned that it was the Goddess?

"Listen, little man, don't piss me off!" She said.

The power in Her voice scared him, just a little.

"Please, let's not make a scene, shall we?" Duane told her, nicely now, looking Her straight in the eye.

"Oh, *we* shall, if I don't get my audition."

Duane and the Goddess went back and forth like that for a few minutes, their voices getting louder by the sentence.

Now, not being able to concentrate on the model strutting on the stage, Tom turned off the music.

"Hold it a minute," he told the model on the stage. "What's going on, over there?" And he quickly walked over to Duane and the Goddess.

"What the hell is going on?" Tom asked in an angry whispered voice. "I'm in the middle of working, here!"

Duane stood and pulled Tom away from where the Goddess stood and spoke in hushed tones.

"I don't know, Mr. Morley. This... woman wants to audition for you. Of course, I told her that was impossible.. She's not a model. I mean, look at her!"

It was then that Tom took a good, long look at the Goddess, who gave him a big smile.

After a moment's thought, Tom made his decision.

"Give her a number, Duane."

"What?!" said his not understanding assistant.

"Listen, she might be from one of those damn feminist groups and I don't need any more trouble! Right now I can't afford to be called sexist in any way, shape or size. Give her a number!"

Tom then returned to the Goddess.

"And what's your name," he asked, sounding overly nice.

"Tara. Just Tara," She replied.

"Well, that's a lovely name," said Tom, trying not to sound patronizing.

"Thank you. It means Earth."

"Oh. Earth. Well, take a seat and it will be your turn in no time."

"Thank you. You're very gracious," She told Tom.

As he walked back to his desk, he said under his breath, "Yeah, lady, I have to be, now."

He turned the music back on and the waiting model starting her strutting, once again.

Finally, the last model finished her audition and was leaving the stage.

'Thank you so much, ah..." Tom said looking at her photo for her name. "...Sloan. Very nice. We'll be in touch."

Knowing what was coming, a few of the models had hung around just to see Tara's audition.

Tom looked around the room, then to the Goddess, who was the only one left sitting in one of the chairs, waiting patiently.

"Tara? Yes, you're up."

The Goddess rose and walked over to him.

"Oh, here is my headshot. Your assistant didn't seem interested in taking it. And would you mind if I used my own music?" She asked, quite politely.

"No, I don't think it'll matter," Tom told Her.

Yes, Tom looked totally bored, like he was simply tolerating the whole situation. And he

185

was also tired, not sure, now, that the model he was looking for had auditioned for him this day.

The Goddess took the stage and nodded to Tom. He put her CD in and a new music started. Suddenly, there was a totally different feeling to the room. The music was beautiful, as if from another time. Flutes, guitars and drum music filled the room. It was native, raw, yet melodic.

At first the Goddess just stood on the stage, not moving, but having a powerful presence. She was calm and She was beautiful, in Her own way. She was filled with dignity. Slowly, She began to move to the music. As She swayed, She was both earthy and sensuous.

And then the music abruptly changed to a much faster beat and the Goddess began to strut *Her* stuff. She pouted. She smiled. She swaggered. She swayed. She kicked. She teased. She hip-hopped. She swiveled. She vogued. She was Madonna, the Black Madonna in all Her glory.

As Tom watched Her, he was mesmerized, by Her looks, by Her movements, by Her mere presence.

When the song ended, the Goddess, as cool as a cucumber, walked off the stage and thanked Tom for the opportunity, then left, without taking Her music CD with Her.

It was night and Tom was alone in his office, sitting on the floor, photos of the models who had auditioned, spread out in front of him. The Goddess's music was playing softly in the background.

Tom stared hard and examined with his professional eye, photo after photo. Some he put in a pile of 'keepers', some he discarded into the trashcan next to him.

He picked up the photo of 'Tara,' and stared and stared at it, remembering Her audition. His body swayed to the music. And he thought for a long time. Then he started to put Her photo into the 'keeper' pile.

"What, am I nuts?" he said out loud, throwing it in the trash.

In a hospital room, the walls painted a light olive green, Harry, his eyes closed, laid on a bed, hooked up to a number of tubes and monitors. Moving his head just a little, a moan emanated from his dry mouth.

A nurse, sitting in a chair near to the bed, got up and went to him.

"Mr. Platt. Can you hear me? How are we feeling? We certainly slept a long time, didn't we?" she asked in her caring nurse voice.

His eyes, opened and he tried to focus on her.

"Am I okay?" he mumbled.

"You're fine, Mr. Platt. The operation is over and you were a real trooper."

"Are... they... there? Did... she... did she... take them, away? My... my...?

"No, Mr. Platt. They're right where they should be. Dr. Hardy removed just the tumor and you are going to be fine."

"Ohhh... tell her, 'thank you,' for... saving my... balls..."

The nurse smiled and checked his I.V. and vital signs.

The door to the room opened and the nurse looked up.

"Oh, isn't this nice, Mr. Platt? You have a visitor."

"Emily? Emily, is that you?' Harry said, trying to raise his head.

Nora walked up to the side of the bed. She was holding a large bouquet of flowers.

"No, Harry, it's me, Nora."

An immediate look of fear crossed over Harry's pale face.

"Get away from me. Don't hurt me. You already ruined my life..." Harry cried, shaking his weak head back and forth.

"Now calm down, Mr. Platt. Everything's fine," the nurse said, as she checked to make sure he hadn't pulled out any of his tubes.

She then leaned over and whispered to Nora. "He's still a little groggy, but he's going to be fine. I'll bring a vase for those beautiful flowers."

The nurse left, as Nora put the flowers down on the nightstand.

"Flowers?" asked Harry.

"Yes, I brought you flowers, Harry. How're you feeling?"

"I feel lousy, Nora. Why are you even here?" he asked, as she handed him a glass of water with a straw to drink out of.

"Well, despite what you think, I'm not really such a terrible person. Listen, Harry, I was never out to ruin you. Just to teach you that you can't treat people the way you do. At least, you can't treat me that way."

"Yeah? Because of you, my Emily left me."

Nora cranked up his bed to a low sitting position, than sat down in the chair.

"No, Harry, she left because of you."

Harry was quiet for a moment, then he took another sip of water.

"Okay, I screwed up, didn't I? I screwed up and I got caught."

"Yes, Harry, you did."

"Know what they almost did to me?" he said, groggily changing the subject.

"I heard." she said, sympathetically.

"It's a scary thing, you know. It really got me where I live."

Nora said nothing, just smiled a tender little smile.

"What am I going to do, Nora? What am I going to do, now? For the first time in my life, I don't know. I've been humbled. My reputation... my wife... it's gone, all gone. And now I almost lost my..."

"You'll figure it out, Harry. Maybe you've already started to."

Harry nodded his still 'fuzzy' head, as Nora leaned over and patted his hand. He held it and squeezed it, lightly, not letting it go.

"Ya know, Nora," he said, still obviously groggy, "way back then, when we were together, I really did love you. I just couldn't leave Emily, though. And my kids. What would they have done without me? But I did really love you."

Nora just nodded her head, realizing that she was getting teary.

"Will you stay here with me, for a little while? I think I don't want to be alone."

Nora just nodded her head, again and pulled her chair closer to his bed.

Harry reached out for her and she again took his hand.

"Sure, Harry. I'll stay with you for a little while."

And they stayed that way, hand in hand, even after Harry fell back to sleep.

CHAPTER FIFTEEN

SHE'S BAAACK!

The sun was rising over the city. A new day had begun in the world and as Tom looked up, he hoped and prayed a new day had begun for him, also. Standing next to him was Duane. They both were looking up at the top of a building, looking up at a covered giant billboard, high in the sky. Workmen were just about to unveil it.

Tom looked very nervous. Duane looked very nervous.

"Mr. Morley, I believe I have been a very good assistant to you all these years, right?"

"You have, Duane. Couldn't ask for a better one,"

"Well, if this new campaign of yours, well, if... if it doesn't do well, that is, as well as you want it to, you will give me good references, won't you?"

"It won't fail, Duane. It can't fail. It just can't."

"But just in case it does, I'll need another job ASAP."

"Ye of little faith, Duane. Of course I'll write a great letter of recommendation for you, although I'm not sure anything I might say, considering, would impress anyone in this business."

"Oh, crap, I never thought of that," said a quickly unhappy Duane.

Just then, the workmen, high on the scaffold, brought down the large sheet covering Tom's new ad. Both Tom and Duane held their breath. People on the street looked up to see what was about to be unveiled.

And there it was for all to see. It was a huge sand colored perfume bottle. In large brown and gold letters over the bottle was the name of the new perfume. EARTH – A MUSK BY THOMAS MORLEY.

Next to the bottle was a face of a black woman, smiling a beautiful and warm smile. Her wild hair had been braided and beaded, African style. Tom's new perfume model was... Tara... the Goddess.

People on the street, especially women, looked up at the new billboard and smiled, because the smile of the Goddess was infectious.

Tom let out the breath he'd been holding in, in anticipation of this moment.

"Well, it's done. It's out there, now," said Tom, himself smiling.

"I want to apologize, Mr. Morley. It's a beautiful ad and Tara, well, Tara is beautiful, too. You were right to pick her."

"Well, sometimes it's good to take a risk, you know? Now we'll just have to wait to see if it pays off," said Tom, nervously. "Okay, on to the next one!"

And they both started walking at a good clip for a couple of blocks.

On another building, another billboard was almost ready to be unveiled. And same as before, Tom and Duane looked nervous, as they paced back and forth, waiting for the huge sheet to be taken off and reveal the essence of Tom's new clothing line.

The sheet finally was brought down and there in living color was the model, the Goddess Tara, once again. In a full length, colored photo,

She was wearing one of Tom's new and beautiful batik dresses. She had one hand on Her rounded and full hip, Her head was thrown back and She was laughing. The ad caption read: FOR THE REAL WOMAN – EARTH FASHIONS BY THOMAS MORLEY.

A crowd of women had gathered, looked up to the ad and immediately started to cheer and applaud.

Seeing this, Tom was completely overwhelmed. Duane slapped Tom's back, happily.

"And to think I was worried," said Duane, giddy with laughter.

"Can't count our chickens, yet, Duane. Let's not celebrate until they start to sell, the clothing and the perfume," Tom told him, although he had a very, very good feeling in his heart.

In Ted's office, Ted was not getting slapped on the back. Oh no, he was slapping his own head, over and over again in outrage, until his halo fell off.

"Oh... my... God!! Oh... my... God!!! Oh my God!!!"

Just then, coughing loudly, God toddled in, slowly.

"You called?" He asked, almost sounding drunk

"Oh God, you're not going to believe what She's done, now!! Look!!!"

God plopped down on a chair and looked at the monitor.

"Wow," He said, His eyes wide, His head still woozy from His cold meds.

"Wow!!?? Wow??!! Whatta ya mean, 'Wow!?'"

"Well, I have to say, I don't think I've ever seen Her look better," said God, His words slurring a bit, as He continued to stare at the TV monitor and cough, at the same time.

"Look better?" now Ted was screaming. "Dear Father, She's up on billboards, selling... stuff! She can't do that!"

God thought for a moment. And then another.

"Well, it isn't as if *I* haven't had my image on everything from, hmm, paintings, to cards, to those mug things to drink out of, to T shirts..."

That voiced reality certainly took Ted by surprise and off his game. He had never thought of that, before. People capitalizing on his boss. Huh. But it was true. The Great Father's likeness certainly did influence people, no doubt about it.

'But, but, that's besides the fact,' Ted, thought, his mind racing.

"But Your Holiness, you are God! It's different!"

God didn't hear Ted, now, for He had dozed off in the chair.

Ted looked at his sleeping God and rolled his eyes. This was all very wrong and as soon as He woke up, Ted would tell Him so. Someone must stop the Goddess! In the meantime, Ted would have to come up with a good reason why.

Sitting on a park bench, the now hugely over-weight Sally was eating a double-decker chocolate ice cream cone with hot fudge and sprinkles on the top of it. She was looking up at Tom's billboard, not knowing quite what to think of it.

'He certainly went in a different direction, that's for sure,' thought Sally. 'It's never gonna fly.'

Some ice cream dripped down onto her rather ugly 'tent' type dress. Pissed, she wiped it off with her free hand, making more of a mess. Disgusted with herself, she got up and threw the remaining cone into a trash bin, but not before taking one more large slurp of it. Now the ice cream was smeared across her face. She wiped her face with the sleeve of her dress. And at that moment, Sally hated herself more than ever.

She then walked away, but turned to take one more look at the Earth Fashion ad and the strange choice Tom had picked to be his model for his new fashion line.

As she continued walking through the park, she passed the hugely pregnant Julie, who was sitting on a bench with Dick. He was licking on an ice cream cone.

Suddenly, Julie's face grimaced in pain.

"Oooooh…!"

"What? What is it? What's the matter?" asked an agitated Dick.

"I think I just had a contraction!"

"You did? Are you sure? Did you? Oh, God, we gotta get to the hospital!" said the near to hysterical daddy-to-be.

But Julie was cool as a cucumber. She had this beautifully serene look on her face, that of a woman about to go through what Mother Nature intended a woman to go through.

"It's okay, Dick. There's nothing to worry about. We have plenty of time."

Dick got up and ran around her like a chicken with its head cut off. He threw his ice cream into a near-by trash bin.

"No! This is it! I know it is! I'll get the car. You call Doctor Lilith! No, wait! You get the car and I'll call her!"

"Dick! Dick! Calm down, please. It's okay. It's okay."

And then, Dick suddenly doubled over in pain.

"Oooh... aaah... Damn! I shouldn't have eaten that ice cream! Didn't our doctor say you shouldn't eat before delivery? Oooh, it hurts. It hurts!" he cried.

Julie shook her pretty head in amusement. Then, struggling some, she got up and took his arm.

"C'mon, Dick, it's going to be okay. Just take deep breaths. Breathe. Breathe."

Dick tried to breath like he had been taught in their Lamaze class, but just couldn't remember exactly how to do it. It was one thing to practice breathing when one wasn't in pain, in labor, but this was different. This hurt.

For the first time in a very long time, Sally ventured into a department store, now looking at all the skinny clothes she could no longer wear. It was so depressing to her, she had to wonder what had possessed her to enter this establishment of fashion, to begin with. But something did. Yes, it hadn't been that long ago that she had loved browsing the clothing aisles, being so very critical, knowing that no other designer could hold a candle to Thomas Morley. And how she had loved seeing the blown-up ads, her ads of his clothes.

She almost bumped into a very thin young woman, picking out some pencil thin skirts to try on. The woman looked Sally up and down in her ice cream stained tent dress and gave her a sympathetic look, Sally was sure of it.

Beyond embarrassed and about to walk out, rather run out of the store and get something to eat, Sally's attention was drawn to a corner of the floor, crowded with shoppers. It was the new Thomas Morley Boutique. Wanting her swollen feet to walk away, they didn't and soon she was in the mist of real women, young and old of all sizes, admiring and trying on Tom's new line. Some of the women, close to where she was standing, were testing his new 'Earth Musk' perfume. The scent made its way into her nostrils. She breathed it in and hated to admit it, but she liked it, liked it very much.

Sally then slowly and rather timidly made her way over to some racks and started looking through the clothes. She took one dress that caught her eye and held it up to her, in front of a mirror. It was a loose fitting dress, made of the softest of fabrics, multi-colored, beige and brown and a light burnt orange, with a hint of yellow running through it.

A few minutes later, she came out of one of the changing rooms wearing the dress and checked herself out in a three-way mirror. After a moment or two of staring at herself, she decided she actually liked it.

A regular sized woman came out of another changing room, wearing another of Tom's designs.

"Aren't these clothes just wonderful," the woman said to Sally.

"Oh. Yes. They're very nice," Sally said back, politely.

"Finally, a clothing designer that understands women. That dress looks terrific on you, by the way. You should buy it," the woman continued. "And what's so great are that the prices are so reasonable. Not like all those high fashion, high end crap you see in all those magazines."

She smiled at the woman and told her she liked the dress she had on, too.

Sally took another look of herself in the mirror and suddenly all her fat didn't look that bad. What was it about this dress, she wondered?

Out of nowhere, Tom came up behind her and she saw his reflection in the mirror. Suddenly, she wished she could just disappear into oblivion. The last thing she had ever wanted was for him to see her looking this way. It never had occurred to her that he might actually be in this store.

"Sally? Sally, is that you?" Tom said.

Sally turned around to him.

"Tom…"

Tom did a very good job hiding any shock he had, seeing her in the shape she was in.

"Wow, how are you? It's been a while." He said genuinely.

"Yes. It has. But I see you're back on top, again. Your clothes are really lovely," she said, now wishing she could simply melt into the floor.

"Thanks. And I love that dress on you."

"Please. Please, Tom, please don't look at me. I know how horrible I look," she said, tears now in her eyes.

"Sal. It's okay. We've all gone through some hard times. Really hard times."

"C'mon, Tom. I don't deserve any kindness from you," she told him.

"What're you talking about?"

"Don't Tom. Please. I bailed on you when you were at your lowest. It was a rotten thing to do and really, I'm ashamed of myself for doing it," she told him, sincerely.

"Ya know what? Ancient history." He looked right in her eyes and then an idea popped into his head. "Come back. Come back and work with me. I could really use you."

"Yeah, right. You look like you're doing just fine without me. And your ads are really wonderful. Where in God's name did you find that model?"

"Tara? Funny thing, she just sort of came out of nowhere at my open call audition. For obvious reasons, I almost didn't use her, even threw her head shot in the trash, but then I just kept thinking about her. I had already started designing the line, but certainly not for someone who looked like her. And then, I don't know, it just all came together for me. And the weirdest thing is her name. Tara. It means Earth."

"Well, she's perfect. Are you going to continue using her?"

"I'd love to, but unfortunately, she left the city. She said she had to go back down... whatever that meant. Maybe she's from Australia, although she doesn't have an accent."

"Well, you'll find someone else."

"Maybe, but it would be great if you came back and helped me do that, find another perfect model."

Now Sally cried in earnest.

"Thank you... okay... okay... thank you, Tom..."

He put his arms around her and they hugged for a long time.

Hiding, a number of feet away, behind another rack filled with Tom clothes, the Goddess and Sophie watched and smiled. And then *they* hugged each other. They looked at each other, nodded, then raced out of the store.

In the maternity ward, Julie was in the delivery room, her feet up in the stirrups. She was in full labor, panting, blowing out, close now to delivering new life. By her side was Nurse Sophie, who was holding her hand and wiping the sweat from her brow. At the end of the delivery table was Doctor Lilith Hardy, the Goddess, constantly giving Julie instructions, helping her to birth her baby.

Dick stood near-by, a pained look on his face.

"Alright, Julie, blow out in rapid breaths. You're doing great," the Goddess told her.

Julie started to pant. So did Dick.

Julie moaned a deep and guttural moan. So did Dick.

"Breath, breath," instructed the Goddess. "That's it. The baby's almost here!"

Julie continued panting. Dick continued panting. Fast and hard.

"Ooooh... I feel faint! I don't feel so good," said Dick between pants and blowing out.

"Not you! Stop it! Stop it!" Sophie told Dick, starting to get annoyed.

"I don't feel so good," Dick said, again.

He started to keel over, but Sophie lightly smacked him on his cheek.

"Hey! Get a grip, idiot!" Sophie told him in no uncertain terms.

Julie continued her panting, so concentrated on this, the most important job of her life, that she would ever have in her life.

"Good, good, Julie. The baby's head has crowned. Now you can push. For ten counts, push!" the Goddess said.

Dick grabbed Julie's hand and held it overly tightly, while watching the overhead mirror and delivery.

"Aaahhh... Mmmmm... Ahhh-ahhhh...," Julie moaned, continuously.

Now Dick was pushing, also. His face was beet red.

"Aarrgghhh... Mmmmm... Aarrghh... I can't do this anymore!" Dick cried "Drugs! Gimme drugs! I need drugs! This is killing me!" screamed Dick.

Sophie smacked him harder, this time on the side of his head. The Goddess gave him a *look*.

"Alright, you can both rest. Take a big cleansing breath, now," the Goddess told them.

If truth be told, the Goddess was getting a very big kick out of watching Dick. Men! Perhaps if all of them went through this, physically, when their wives were delivering babies, maybe they'd appreciate women more, She thought.

Dick took a very deep breath, but the poor guy looked like he was going to pass out. On the other hand, as hard as she was working, Julie was incredibly calm, having only one thing on her mind, to deliver her baby.

"Okay, time to push, again," the Goddess told Julie, after checking the baby's progress, coming into this world. "I think this will be it. Big breath and… push!"

Julie and Dick both took deep breaths and pushed very hard.

Julie moaned.

Dick screamed.

"No more! No more! I can't take anymore of this!" yelled Dick, as if he were dying.

At this critical point in the delivery, even Julie looked over to her husband. Then she raised her hand and smacked him in the face.

"Dick! Hello?!" she managed as she pushed and pushed.

"C'mon, Julie. This is it! Push!" the Goddess told Her patient. "Dick! Help you wife!!"

"Yeah! Help your wife, for crying out loud." This from Nurse Sophie.

And so it was that some kind of sanity finally came over Dick. His eyes became clear and finally he focused, not on himself, but on his wife.

"Okay, okay. C'mon, Honey, push. Push! You can do it. You can do it. I know you can!" he told Julie.

"Push, Julie, push!" said the Goddess and Sophie, at the same time.

"Push, Honey. If I could, I'd do it for you. I swear, I would. Push!" Dick told her.

And Julie pushed and pushed and pushed.

"One more, Julie! One more big push!" the Goddess told her.

"Push, Darling!" Dick told her.

And Julie, exhausted, but so excited, pushed.

"Here it comes... And... we have a baby, folks! And it's a girl!" the Goddess told them.

Then She gently took the newborn and laid her on Julie's breast, for those first, important moments of bonding. There were tears in Julie's eyes, as she gently stroked her new baby's little head.

"I did it. I just had a baby," Julie cried, emotionally.

Trembling, Dick touched his baby girl's little hand and then doing exactly what the Goddess told him, he cut the cord. He then leaned over and kissed his wife, again and again, pride busting out of him.

The Goddess and Sophie looked at the new family, then their eyes met each other and they smiled and nodded.

"Oh, Dick, look. She's so beautiful," Julie told Dick, through tears.

"We did it! I mean, you did it. Wow! Holy cow. Oh, man, our baby girl. I love you, Julie. I love you so much," said the weeping Dick.

"I can't believe she's really here..." said Julie.

"Let's name her Lilith, after Doctor Hardy," Dick told her, emotionally overcome.

"Yes! Lilith. And maybe Lily for short."

All during Julie's pregnancy, the two had fought over names, never having found one they both loved. But in an instant, that had changed.

"Did you know that Lilith was a mid-eastern Goddess," the Goddess told the two. "She had wings and a crown."

"Then Lilith it is!" said Dick. "She'll be better than just an old princess. She'll be a Goddess!"

And they all laughed.

The Goddess then picked up the child, one of Her namesakes and held her in the air, just the way that elder Crone had done in the cave, so many eons ago. And baby Lilith gave out her first cry of life.

CHAPTER SIXTEEN

<u>THE GODDESS AND GOD</u>

In Her Realm, the Goddess was feeling fit, fantastic and feisty, like a new woman, a woman reborn, beautiful and empowered.

With the money She had made from Her 'Tara' Earth Fashions and Perfume ads, She donated it to Planned Parenthood, Women's Homeless Shelters and to the women folk who lobbied Congress for women's equality on a number of issues.

She knew that during Her time up on... Her, She had made a difference, albeit a small one. But it was a start and She knew, if change was going to come, it had to start somewhere.

The Goddess and Sophie were lugging a large picnic basket, each holding onto its handles on either side of the basket, as they walked through the tall grasses of Her Realm. They were on their way to what, at least, the Goddess hoped would be a feast of some significance.

"Well, I have to say, mission accomplished, Your Goddessliness!" Sophie told Her, happily.

"Not quite, my faithful friend. A work in progress might be a better way to put it. There's still so much to do. A woman's work is never done. And like I said, before, if I have to do it one person at a time, well, that's what I'll do. But I must tell you, you made one terrific judge! I think you were really in your element."

"Hey, maybe I could get my own TV show, huh? Judge Sophie!!"

"Well, you'd have a lot of competition, what with all those Judge Judy knock-offs, these days," the Goddess laughed. "Although I surely would have loved to see poor Harry squirm like he did, in front of a nationwide audience."

Thinking about it, the Goddess was quite happy with the results of Her recent labor.

Dick had turned out to be quite a wonderful father to little Lily, getting up at night and bringing the child to her mother's breast for her sustenance, rocking her to sleep when she was cranky, so Julie could rest. He never entered a strip bar, again, either, cringing at the thought that one day, his beautiful little daughter could or would ever choose to dance like that for men, as a career.

After watching Julie give birth, he acquired a whole new respect for her and for women in general. Yes, he still watched his favorite football team play on Sunday afternoons, but he no longer yelled obscenities, when the opposing team made a touchdown... not while holding his baby in his arms, that was for sure.

Julie couldn't believe the change in her husband, of course, never having the slightest notion what it was that had precipitated this drastic change in him.

She was sad when she learned Doctor Lilith Hardy had left her practice, especially since Julie wanted to get pregnant within a reasonable period of time, to give her Lily a sibling. The word in her gyno's office was that Doctor Hardy was going to follow a lifelong dream of climbing the Himalayan Mountains. Something about wanting to 'get back to the earth.'

Harry slowly recovered from his surgery, glad to be alive, even more glad to have his balls intact. Although they weren't rushing into anything, he and Nora were seeing each other, reconnecting, Nora trying to understand her old lover of long ago and why he had made the choices he had made. He profusely apologized to her, over and over again and eventually, she forgave him, for not leaving Emily for her, for not making her Partner, for not realizing the important things in this life.

Yes, almost losing one's balls was definitely enough to change a man, but even more so, while he recuperated, it gave him time to reassess his life and reassess he did. He disbanded what was left of his law firm and sold his mansion. After many hours and days and weeks of discussion, Nora convinced him to join her in her new, small law firm that would only take on cases advocating for women's reproductive and equality rights and injustices that affected all minorities.

It was a new day, a new life for Harry Platt and he hoped soon, he would convince her to became one Ms. Nora Abrams Platt. No, love does *not* mean 'never having to say you're sorry.' Love means owning up to what you did, how you have behaved and lived your life, seeing the errors of your ways and grow and learn and change... and that is love. And Harry was trying his damnedest to be a changed man.

And as for Tom, well, his Earth clothing and perfume lines were a fantastic success, in fact, slowly other designers even started trying to copy him. But they were never able to perfect a scent anything close to Earth Musk, much less replicate the soul of his batik clothing.

Sally, working again with Tom, did lose a good portion of her weight, but not all of it. She was down to a healthy size ten and liked herself much more than when she had just allowed herself to nibble on grapes and berries, to keep herself skinny.

And women, real women, so appreciated Tom's clothes. No matter what size they were, they knew they could slip on his dresses and tops and feel beautiful and sensuous. Even Whoopi Goldberg started wearing Thomas Morley designs everyday on The View, which bolstered sales to an even higher degree.

And as the Goddess and Sophie continued walking through the tall grasses, they felt hope in their hearts. But there was still some unfinished business to deal with.

"So, do we really have to do this?" asked Sophie of the Great Mother.

"We do, my little Sophie. It's the next step," the Great Mother replied.

Walking slowly on Heaven's side of the line was God and Ted, His angel, who wasn't feeling very ambitious at that moment. God continually coughed and coughed, the congestion in His chest, worse than ever.

"So, do we really have to do this?" Ted asked of His Holiness.

"I think we do, Ted. Now just try and control your anger and let's see if we can get to the bottom of all this. I don't know why She's been doing what She's been doing, but I aim to find out." And then He started hacking, again.

When God and Ted got to that place, that line that separated Heaven and Earth, they saw that the Goddess and Sophie were already there. On the ground, overlapping across that line, a red and white checkered blanket was laid out. On it was a virtual feast the women had prepared. Berries and nuts, fresh fruit and veggies. And especially for God, lox, cream cheese and bagels, which the Goddess knew was His favorite.

The men sat down on their white side, Ted giving Sophie the evil eye, which she immediately gave back to him. But he was rather famished and dug into the turkey sandwich she had made especially for him, even though Sophie had hated every minute of doing it.

And for a long while, they all ate in silence.

"So…" started the Goddess.

"So…" God said back.

"So, what do you think?" She went on.

"Think? I don't know what to think. I think, I know, well, I think I know, you overstepped your bounds, Mother. Yes, I do." He told Her.

"No, no, a mother can never overstep her bounds. And when the children look back on it, they always have to admit, their mother was right," She said, knowing She was right.

Ted rolled his eyes.

"Hey, sonny! Don't you roll your eyes at Mother!" Sophie hissed at Ted.

The look on Sophie's face made Ted recoil just a tad. He didn't like not being in control. He didn't like being reprimanded by her. No, he definitely didn't like this ancient person, at all. 'Who, in God's name did she think she was, anyway?' he thought.

Ignoring her, Ted took a big handful of grapes to munch on.

"Could ya save some for the rest of us? Whatta ya think, this stuff grows on trees?" hissed Sophie, again.

Almost timidly, Ted put some of the grapes back onto the picnic blanket.

"Like I'm really gonna eat that after you touched them grapes with your grubby little hands!"

"Sorry…" said Ted.

"Enough, you two," said God, having yet another coughing attack.

"You sound terrible. Worse than before. What's wrong with you?" asked the Goddess, truly concerned.

"Just choked. Just choked," He said, continuing to cough.

"Well, I think I know something that can help you," the Goddess told him, knowingly.

And with that, She pulled Him over to Her side of the line, where the earth was rich and the grass grew high.

"No! No! Whatta ya doing, nu?" God said, struggling to crawl back to Heaven's side.

"Shhh… Don't worry. Mother knows what's best," She told Him, gently.

Considering She was so much stronger than Him, it was no contest, as She virtually dragged Him away.

Seeing this, Ted went bonkers, yelling, screaming at the Goddess to bring Him back, bring Him back, doing anything he could to save his boss, except crossing that line. Sophie, getting an extreme headache from the little twit's yelling and screaming, reached over the line and smacked him on the side of the head.

"Will you shut-up!!," she screamed back at him. "The forces of nature have shifted, so you had better get used to it!"

Ted, not having any idea what was going on or what she was talking about, cowered, his angel wings drooping some.

"Now sit down!" Sophie told him.

Ted did as he was told. He sat.

"Here. Have a grape." And she handed him one.

The Goddess and God walked for a while, He, in his weakened state, leaning on Her.

"It's nice here," God told Her, as he noticed all the trees and flowers and animals scurrying about.

"Yes, it is," was all She said.

Soon they were at their destination at one of the Goddess's marvelous hot springs. Although He fought Her tooth and nail, She took off His toga and within minutes they were both submerged in the steaming water, which was up to their naked shoulders.

"Mm... this does feel good."

"Thank you," She said, smiling at Him.

"Oy, ya know, I just don't understand it. In over six thousand years, I've never so much as had a sniffle. Why? Why? Why?!" He cried.

"So, when did it start, Daddy, you not feeling well?" She asked, already knowing.

"I don't know..." And He thought and thought. "Wait! Ted was right. I've been so out of it on meds, I forgot. It was, yes, it was when *you* started sticking your nose into my business, that's when."

The Goddess just smiled Her strong and ethereal smile at Him.

"What? No?" God questioned.

"Well, maybe now you can imagine how I've felt for all these years."

"Huh?" He said, with a blank look on His face.

"You know, getting weaker and weaker."

"But, but, you look quite sensational now. How did you get well again?" God asked in all earnestness.

"I took control back, that's how. I demanded to be seen and heard, my way. I made the decision that I wasn't just going to just die out, to be forgotten," She told Him.

"Oh... Well, I would have never forgotten you."

"What a sweet thing to say, Father. Ya know, I've been doing a lot of thinking, about you, about me and I think it's time for us to call a truce."

"A truce? Whatta ya mean?" He asked.

"A truce. Armistice? Peace? The world is big enough for both of us, you know."

"I thought they were all doing just fine and dandy, before you came back, before you reeked such crazy stuff on them… and me, too. And oy, I've been feeling so bad. So bad."

"It's all in your mind, Daddy. They don't have to make a choice between us. But they should just know about me, too. And then they can honor both of us in their own ways. You know, look up to both of us," She told him.

Even in the hot springs, She towered over the little man.

"Okay, okay, they look *up* to you, but they look up to you *on* me! They just have to be reminded of that fact. They have to remember to love their Mother, also," She went on.

"So, so, what're you saying?"

"What I'm saying is that we should work together for the greater good. Maybe then they'd work together, better."

God thought about that a while.

"Despite what you think, I don't think they're inherently bad, just uneducated, at least when it comes to me," She said.

"Sometimes when it comes to me, too," he admitted.

"Yes, that is true. The things they do in your name. They fight, they kill, they profess that *their* God is better than other's God. They use your name for their wars, for their prejudices. It's quite sad. But they can learn. I think I proved that to be so," She said, as Her hot springs swirled around them.

Although, in Her heart, She wondered and worried if they could, indeed, learn, the masses, that is. And if they did not learn and learn quickly, they all might well destroy each other and themselves, in the process. This was not the way it was supposed to be, the Goddess thought. No, not the way it was supposed to be, at all. Next time, She would work on hate and prejudice. But then there was the environment, the one percent versus the ninety-nine percent, immigration, worker's rights, oh my. So many problems, so little time.

"I haven't been paying enough attention to them…" God said rather sadly.

"Now, don't do a poor, poor pitiful me, thing. You've really done a lot of good. You've given them faith and hope and forgiveness."

"Well, that's the nicest thing you've said to me in a very long time. Actually, ever! And, don't tell anyone I said it, especially not Ted, but you're not so bad, yourself. You're... earthy. I like that in a woman."

Suddenly, the Goddess got very shy and blushed through Her dark skin.

"Oh, you... Really?" She said coyly.

"Yes! And I admit it, there has been a lack of respect and recognition for you the last couple of thousand years. I think that must change!" He told Her.

"Well, well, well, will surprises never cease."

"Yes! Yes! I decree it! We should start working together from now on! Ya did good with them, Ma."

"Well, thank you, Pa."

"This is strange, but I think I'm already feeling a little better. I haven't hacked or coughed at all in the last eighteen and a half minutes."

"It's my healing powers, don't ya know?" She said.

And then they smiled warmly at each other, the Mother and the Father.

"Okay, okay," said the now slightly embarrassed God. "Enough of this sappy stuff, nu? What's for dinner? I hope not fish, again."

"And what's wrong with my fish? You don't like my fish?"

"I didn't say that. Now don't get all sensitive on me. I just thought something else would be nice, for a change, that's all."

"Well, maybe you'd get what you like if *you* cooked, once in a while. Ever think of that?"

"What, you don't think I know how to cook?"

"Oh, do you?"

"I happen to be a very good cook. Ask Ted," He said, getting defensive, now.

"Yeah? So, what are you going to cook *me* for dinner, huh?"

They then looked at each other, this big, black woman of the earth and the little man from Heaven and they laughed.

Hours later, as the sun was setting, found the Goddess and God back on either side of their line, ready to take their leave of each other, at least for now.

"Dance with me," said God.

"Dance with you?" She repeated, surprised.

And God took Her hand from across that line that separated them and the two started doing their old favorite dance from the 50's, *The Stroll*, made so popular on Dick Clark's American Bandstand.

And so it was, the Mother and the Father, together, strolled into the sunset... which Sophie made sure set right on time.

And no, my children, fear not, for this is not the end, but hopefully the beginning of a new and wonderful (and equal) relationship between woman and man.

CPSIA information can be obtained
at www.ICGtesting.com
Printed in the USA
FSOW04n0847090316
17832FS